FABLE
OF EYLAN

A NOVEL

MAKING A DIFFERENCE, ONE BOOK AT A TIME

In the belief that we can make a difference together, a portion of the proceeds from the sale of this book will be donated to GRRAND (Golden Retriever Rescue & Adoption of Needy Dogs) in Louisville, Kentucky.

This cause is close to my heart, and your support helps us contribute to meaningful change in the lives of countless dogs.

Thank you for being a part of this journey!

FABLE

OF EYLAN

BOOK TWO

A TAIL OF FLAME AND STORM

H. R. HUTZEL

A TAIL OF FLAME AND STORM: FABLE OF EYLAN (BOOK TWO)

Copyright © 2024 by H. R. Hutzel

ISBN: 979-8-9892253-2-3

Published by Red Golden Publishing

Printed in the United States of America

Also in the Fable of Eylan series:

A Tail of Wind and Ice (Book One)
ISBN: 979-8-9892253-1-6

A Tail of Magic and Love (Book Three)
ISBN: 979-8-9892253-3-0

Find out more at hrhutzel.com

Get a free digital album, featuring mesmerizing character art and magical scenes from the series!

Download it at
hrhutzel.com/lookbook

To my boys,
Westen, Finnley, Huxley, and Rowan.

May your legacy of love live on, embodied in me
and through these stories.
You are my heart.

Good dogs are with us for a little while to teach us how to love like it's our job, because it is.

—*Unknown*

CHAPTER ONE

ICY WIND WHIPPED NORA'S FACE AND TUGGED at her braided hair. She hunkered forward on Arcturus's back, then dared a glance over the side of his enormous body, seeing nothing but open sky below. She swallowed and turned her attention to Fable, who lay in front of her across the griffin's back as it flew through the midnight-blue skies of Coeur. Rowan rode in front of Fable, both dogs secured with the leather straps of the riding harness Arcturus wore. Nora sat on a small saddle with another thick strap of leather around her waist, binding her to the sky lion. When Arcturus had insisted he'd fly them to the next oracle, she'd almost refused to get on his back. But after seeing Fable and his condition, Nora knew she had to get him help—and quickly.

Rowan, on the other hand, had no fear of climbing onto the giant chimera's back and rode with his head held high, admiring the piercing stars that dotted a now cloudless sky. He still wore the coat Cassian had wrapped him in. The gold aureus hung from the red rope around his neck and glimmered against the forest-green fabric.

Nora shivered as another frigid gust sliced through her woolen tunic. She'd wrapped her cloak around Fable. He needed it more than she did.

Rowan turned to check on his brother, a worried expression tugging at his round eyebrows. He caught Nora's stare, his eyes asking the same questions that spun through her mind. Questions she wanted to ask Fable.

Why was he here?

How was he here?

And what had the queen done to him?

He looked so weak, so frail.

But he was alive.

She leaned farther forward and pressed her body against Fable's, trying to transfer some warmth to him. As she did, she buried her face in the exposed coppery fur of his neck and breathed in his familiar scent. Tears stung her eyes and seeped into his fur as she felt his heartbeat against her own chest.

He was alive.

Fable was alive.

An hour later, after flying farther and farther north, Arcturus broke his silence.

"Were coming upon our destination. It won't be long now."

The sprawling range of the Rasalas mountains continued in front of them, zigzagging across the land. Moonlight glimmered on the snow-crested peaks.

Nora shifted in the saddle and cast a glance over her shoulder, thinking of Cassian, Eira, and Taran. She hoped they were okay. Especially Cassian. He'd insisted that Arcturus take Nora and her dogs to the oracle while he waited with Eira and Taran for the griffin to return for them. An image of his face appeared in her mind, his lips blue, skin reddened with cold. Eira and Taran assured Nora they'd help to keep him warm. But it would still be another couple of hours before they were all reunited.

Nora glanced down at Fable as Arcturus swooped through the sky, and knew they'd made the right call. Her dog's chest rose and fell with short, shallow breaths.

She swallowed against the rising waves of anxiety.

She couldn't lose him.

Not again.

"Hold on," Arcturus said as he soared straight toward one of the mountains.

Nora tightened the leather straps that secured her and her dogs. A narrow cleft became visible in the silvery peak.

Arcturus banked right, angling his body with wings pointed up and down to glide through the split.

The sudden vertical angle caused Nora and her dogs to shift, but the harness held firm. As did the sensation of the bond that surged between her and Rowan, though it wasn't visible at the moment. She held her breath as they entered the narrow gap. The sky lion glided through the fissure, unable to flap his wings in the narrow passage.

A sliver of moonlight beckoned them forward. And moments later, they were out in the open air. Nora exhaled, then gasped.

A glass-like lake stretched in front of them. Starlight reflected off its surface and illuminated the small snow-covered islands that dotted the water, their gentle mounds topped with soaring, white-tipped conifers.

Arcturus swooped low, gliding mere feet above the smooth water. Ahead, orbs of flickering light became visible on the island, like candles visible through the windows of a home. More appeared, then others. And Nora realized she was seeing a small village.

Soaring mountains, nearly as tall as Mount Croia, embraced the lake and its residents on all sides, making the altitude far too great for visibility from above. Nora scanned the fairy-tale landscape. No one could find them here unless they knew to enter through the cleft in the mountain.

Water rushed beneath them as Arcturus glided toward the largest island. Gentle waves crashed against an icy, pebbled beach where a small bonfire flickered in the snow, illuminating the subtle outline of an approaching figure.

Arcturus angled his wings to slow his speed and extended his taloned lion paws for their landing. They stopped without so much as a bump. The griffin shook out his feathery mane, then lowered his belly to the ground so Nora could dismount. She unstrapped herself first, then Rowan, then carefully released the leather bindings that held Fable.

His body, thinner than normal, easily slid off the sky lion's back and into her arms. She lowered him to the ground.

Approaching footsteps crunched in the snow. Two sets. But when Nora glanced up, only one figure appeared. She stiffened when the firelight illuminated the half man, half horse—a centaur, if she remembered her Greek mythology correctly.

"Arcturus?" the creature asked. "Is that you?"

"Hello, my old friend," the griffin replied. "It's been a while."

"A while?" The centaur chuckled. "It's been ages."

The centaur's hooved feet halted. He peered down at Nora, who gripped Fable.

She stared up at the sleek tawny body of a stallion that merged at the chest with the torso of a man. He wore a tunic of thick fur on his upper body, a silver breastplate over it. Icy wind tugged at the loose tendrils of his long black hair, which he'd tied back from his dark face. A scorpion's tail curled behind him, emerging from the horse's rump.

Rowan jumped in front of Nora and Fable, body rigid. The hairs on the back of his neck stood up, and a low growl rumbled in his chest.

"Easy, Red," Arcturus said. "You're safe here. I promise."

Rowan's posture softened, but the hairs between his shoulder blades didn't lower.

The centaur faced Arcturus and placed one of his human hands on the griffin's forehead. Arcturus closed his eyes and drew in a long breath.

"It's good to be home." Arcturus sighed and opened his saffron eyes.

The centaur removed his hand and nodded. "And if you're home, then it can only mean one thing . . ." His voice trailed off as he turned to stare at Nora and her dogs.

"This is Nora," Arcturus said slowly. "And Rowan and Fable." He cleared his throat. "Nora, meet Edric."

The human-hybrid bowed his head and hinged slightly at the waist, right where it connected to his horse body. "It's a pleasure to meet you, Nora."

She chewed her lip and reached for Rowan, pulling him closer to her and Fable. "You too," she said tensely, unable to hide the uncertainty in her voice.

"I have much to tell you," Arcturus said to Edric.

The centaur shifted. "As do I. A lot has changed while you've been away."

Arcturus nodded. "Yes, but later. Right now we need to get this young lady to the oracle. And her . . . Fable needs a healer."

"Of course." Edric motioned to Fable. "May I?"

Before Nora could respond, he stooped to pick him up. She started to protest, but Rowan let out a fierce bark.

Edric backed away. "I'm just trying to help." He pointed to the flickers of light up the pebbled beach. With her eyes adjusted, Nora could now see a small A-frame cottage that sat at the edge of the evergreen tree line. "It's not a far walk, but far enough. Someone must carry him."

Nora stroked Rowan's back. "He's right," she said. She glanced at Arcturus, who gave her a reassuring nod. "Thank you for your help, Edric."

He offered a soft smile, then scooped Fable up into his strong human arms.

"You can trust him," Arcturus said. "You can trust everyone here."

Nora nodded.

"Now, if you're quite all right, I'll return for Cassian and the other Reds."

"We'll be okay," Nora said with a glance at Fable.

"Good. Get some rest. I shall see you in the morning."

And with that, he was off.

Nora watched Arcturus leap into the air, wings beating, carrying him higher and higher, until he was little more than a speck against the moon.

"This way," Edric said and started up the beach.

Rowan followed as close as possible to the centaur, eyes glued to Fable. Nora pushed up from the ground, body weary, then trailed Edric and

Rowan up the frozen pebbled beach toward the cottage.

Once on the porch, the centaur shifted Fable in his arms and knocked on the front door.

Nora puffed warm air into her cupped hands, then patted Rowan's head. "You okay?"

He peered up at her with his soulful brown eyes. "I'll be okay once I know Fable is okay."

She scratched behind his ear and swallowed another swelling wave of dread. "Me too."

A long pause lingered between them before Rowan lowered his voice and said, "I thought we weren't going to see Fable again."

Before Nora could respond, she heard the door swing open. But when she turned, the door remained closed. Light drew her attention downward where a miniature door, built into the full-sized one, stood open, a cottontail rabbit silhouetted in the amber glow.

"Edric!" the female rabbit said. "Do you know what hour it is? Surely your visit could've waited till morn—" The rabbit froze. Her tiny pink nose quivered as she sniffed the air and adjusted the silk sleep bonnet she wore over her ears. She reached into the breast pocket of her matching pajamas, pulled out a tiny pair of glasses, and perched them on the bridge of her nose.

"Heavens!" She backed away from the door. "Get them inside! Quickly!"

Edric turned the handle of the full-sized door and stepped inside carrying Fable. His hooves clomped against the wooden floorboards. Nora and Rowan followed, careful to avoid his scorpion tail.

The rabbit scurried into the cottage's main room. "Place him here." She pointed to a human-sized couch. "Near the fire."

Edric laid Fable on the sofa, which sat perpendicular to the hearth. The rabbit immediately began fussing over Fable, yanking a blanket over his thin body, then touching her small paw to his nose. She felt his ears next, then his feet. "More blankets," she mumbled to no one in particular, then scurried toward a back room.

Nora let out a shaky breath, feeling the warmth of the fire thaw her body. She scanned the cottage, noting the strange mix of full-sized and miniature furniture. The A-frame opened directly into a cozy living space, a tiny kitchen to the left. Above, Nora could make out the faint outlines of a dark loft in the rafters. The fire popped, causing her to jump.

The rabbit returned carrying a small stack of blankets, which she promptly draped over Fable's body.

Without a glance in his direction, she said to Edric, "Get Numair and Althea. Hurry!"

Edric signaled silently to Nora that he'd be right back, then strode out the front door, pulling it closed behind him.

The rabbit paid no attention to Nora and Rowan as she adjusted the blankets on Fable's body, then placed another log on the fire. She hummed as she worked, then sang quietly as she stroked her tiny paw across his forehead.

"Is he going to be okay?" Rowan asked.

The rabbit startled. "Heavens! I forgot you were here!" She stepped away from the couch, still wearing her tiny silk pajamas. She pulled the bonnet from her head, revealing long, pink-lined ears. "Forgive my appearance." She smoothed a paw over her buttercup-yellow pajama shirt. "I wasn't expecting visitors."

"You're the oracle?" Nora asked.

The rabbit nodded. "One of three," she said. "Orella." She held out her paw to shake Nora's hand. "And you are . . . ?"

"Nora."

Orella yanked her paw away. "Oh!"

Nora snatched her hand to her chest. "What?"

Orella glanced between Nora and Rowan, then back at Fable. "Oh my," she said. "It's happening."

The rabbit paced in front of the fireplace, then scurried toward the kitchen area. "Food," she mumbled. "We need food." Louder, she said, "Make yourselves comfortable by the fire. I'll be right back."

Nora stripped off her boots, groaning as she flexed her weary toes. She plopped down on the floor beside the couch where Fable slept, then called Rowan to her and removed his coat. He shook as if shaking off water, then sat beside the couch, his chin resting on the cushion, eyes fixed on his brother. Nora drew her knees to her chest and leaned back against the front of the sofa. A tingling sensation spread through her limbs as the heat from the fire seeped into her bones. Again she thought of Cassian, hoping he could hold on until Arcturus returned for them.

She stroked Rowan's head, but his eyes remained locked on Fable. She could see the mounting questions in his expression, mirroring her own. Pushing herself up to her knees, she faced the couch, then touched a tentative hand to Fable's cheek. A sob caught in the back of her throat. It broke free. Rowan pressed his body against Nora's. Tears slid down her cheeks.

She never thought she'd see Fable again.

Never thought she'd hold him again.

And yet here he was.

The joy of seeing him alive mingled with the sickening fear that she was about to lose him again.

"I have some leftover stew." Orella's voice interrupted Nora's thoughts. "I can throw it over the fire, but it'll take a moment to heat. In the meantime, here's some bread and butter to tide you over."

Nora turned to see the rabbit carrying a small wooden serving board.

"Oh no!" the rabbit exclaimed. "No, no, no!" She set the tray on a miniature side table. "You're crying. Please don't cry." She rushed to Nora's side and touched her arm. "The Red will be fine. You got here just in time."

Nora sniffed and wiped her face. "Really?"

Orella glanced at Fable. "Yes, I think so. I mean, he needs a healer, but . . . yes, he should be just fine." Her eyebrows darted up as if she had an idea. She grabbed a slice of bread from the serving tray, then returned to the couch, where she waved the warm buttered bread in front of Fable's nose. A moment later, he sniffed the air, then licked his lips. Drool dribbled from his mouth.

"You see," Orella said, breaking off the tiniest bite. "He has an appetite. That's a good sign." She popped the piece of bread into Fable's mouth. He swallowed without chewing.

A sob choked Nora's laugh. She stroked Fable's fur. "I can't believe he's alive."

Rowan licked her cheek.

Orella fetched the serving tray and placed it in front of Rowan and Nora, who gobbled down the entire loaf in minutes. The stew Orella had promised didn't take long to heat and tasted even better than the clover stew Finneas had served.

Nora spooned the last few bites into her mouth, watching as Orella ladled a small amount onto a platter, then placed it in front of Fable. He propped his head up to take a couple laps of the stew, then flopped back against the couch, exhausted.

The rabbit touched his nose once more. "He's already warming up," she said. "But his Eylan is quite weak. Undetectable, in fact." She glanced over her shoulder.

Nora shifted.

"But *his* . . ." Orella's soft black eyes found Rowan. Her pink nose quivered as she sniffed. "We haven't seen one of your kind in years."

A knock at the door interrupted them.

"Come in," Orella said.

Nora glanced across the room to the front door, framed by the A-frame's large triangular windows. Edric entered, followed by a female human-hybrid and a Red.

The dog crossed the room and went immediately to Fable's side. The woman paused at the door, slowly pushing it closed with human hands until the latch clicked. Firelight warmed her ebony skin and glinted in her yellow cat eyes. The tight black curls on her head were cut short, nearly to the scalp, revealing the rounded ears of a panther. She walked upright on hind paws as she entered. A long tail emerged from under the hem of her tunic dress and curled behind her.

"Is it true?" the woman asked. The white tips of her elongated canines peeked out from her lips. As she drew near, Nora noted the whiskers that framed her mouth.

"It seems so," Orella said.

"Arcturus brought them?"

Orella nodded.

Nora tried to cling to Arcturus's assurances that everyone on this island was safe, but it was hard when a half-human, half-panther stalked toward her.

Then again, what did she really know about Arcturus? It suddenly occurred to Nora that this could all be a trap, a ploy of Queen Kierra.

"Who are you?" Nora asked. "And what is this place?"

The woman's cream-colored tunic swished as she approached, revealing massive hind paws with equally large claws.

"My name is Numair," the woman purred. "And this part of Coeur doesn't have an official name because the rest of the kingdom doesn't know it exists."

Her words provided no reassurance.

"But over the years we've come to call it Arcadia. More importantly, we call it home." Her lips curled into a feline smile. "This"—she gestured to the Red who was intently sniffing Fable—"is Althea. My dog."

Nora furrowed her brow. "*Your* dog?"

Numair nodded. "Yes, Althea and I were bonded many years ago, when I used to be an Eylan mystic—a trainer and teacher in the great ways of the Eylan."

Nora's head spun. "But now you're a—"

"A chimera, yes. My Eylan was tainted when I was bitten during a raid. Those details don't matter, though. What matters is that you're here now. And we've been waiting for you." She glanced at Fable, then Rowan. "We've been waiting a very long time." She noted the gold medallion around Rowan's neck, then approached with reverent steps. She took a knee before him and held out a hand.

Rowan sniffed her palm once, twice, then offered a lick.

"An aureus," she murmured. "May I?"

Rowan lifted his chin so she could examine it.

Numair drew in a sharp breath as she lifted the coin-sized medallion. "Blessed are you, great Eidolon of Coeur."

Rowan's lips tugged with a tentative smile.

"What should I call you?" she asked.

Rowan's eyes shifted to Nora's.

"Go on," she said to him.

His tail swished. "My name is Rowan!" he said excitedly, the hesitation vanishing. "And that's my human, Nora." He paused, his voice falling slightly. "And this is my brother, Fable. Can you fix him? Please?"

The female Red, Althea, answered. "Yes. I do believe I can. Though it may take all night."

"All night? Shall I fetch more food?" Orella asked.

"That won't be necessary," Numair said. "Althea and I will stay up with Fable. Nora and Rowan should get some rest."

"And I'll be leaving," Edric added. "I must return to my post."

"More blankets, then," Orella said and scurried off to find them.

Edric opened the door to let himself out.

"Wait," Nora said.

The centaur paused. "Yes?"

"What about Arcturus? He'll be returning soon with two other Reds and a boy. They're with us."

"Then I will bring them straight here."

"Thank you," Nora said. She wanted to say more but just repeated, "Thank you."

Edric dipped his head in a small bow, then exited the cottage.

Orella returned a moment later with another stack of blankets and spread them along the floor beside the fire.

She gestured for Rowan and Nora to make themselves comfortable. "Snuggle in, you two. The nights are cold here, as you've surely seen. And they only get colder."

Nora's gut twinged with worry for Cassian.

But it was quickly forgotten as she watched Althea climb onto the couch with Fable.

"What are you doing?"

"I'm a healer," Althea said. "His Eylan is drained. I'll use mine to revive his, like kindling to a small ember."

Nora nodded. "Is there anything we can do? Anything *I* can do?"

"Just rest," Numair said.

Nora settled onto the floor, pulling the blankets as close to the couch as possible while remaining out of Althea's way.

She stared at the still body of her dog. She could just barely see his chest rise and fall beneath the blankets Orella had piled on top of him. Once again, she felt so helpless.

A wave of emotions hurtled into her, mingling with a level of exhaustion she'd never felt. Silent tears streamed down her cheeks as she recalled the moment she'd witnessed Fable collapse onto her kitchen floor, the sound of his body hitting the hardwood an echo that would resonate in her soul for eternity.

Despite Althea's reassurances, she couldn't shake the thought that she was about to lose him again.

Rowan curled up against Nora. Together they watched as Althea grabbed the blankets with her teeth and slowly uncovered Fable. She settled onto the couch, covered his body with hers, then fell eerily still.

A subtle hum filled the room.

Then a warm, golden glow.

Waves of liquid-light pulsed around Althea's body in ebbing and flowing ripples. Surging, then subsiding; growing, then fading; casting eerie shadows along the walls.

Numair patted her dog on the head, then took a seat in one of the human-sized armchairs across from the couch. She leaned back and sighed. Two creases formed between her brows.

"Thank you," Nora said. "I'm sure you were asleep when Edric called on you. We're grateful you came to help us."

The creases in Numair's brow softened. "It's my honor to be here," she said. "Althea's too."

"And mine." Orella appeared at Nora's side and handed her a warm cup of tea. "After all, we've been waiting for you."

"That's what Princess Sadie said. That's what everyone keeps saying." Nora sipped the tea— dandelion root, if she wasn't mistaken, sweetened with a bit of honey. The earthy flavor grounded Nora, though the world around her seemed to spin.

"Yes," Numair said. "Princess Sadie, the Reds, all of the dog packs—they've been waiting for you. But we have too. We've longed for this moment for many years."

Nora took another slow sip, feeling the warmth seep into her body and lull her into a sleepy trance.

"Who's *we*?" she asked.

Numair's mouth parted with a genuine but fanged smile. "Why the Rebellion, of course."

CHAPTER TWO

NORA STIRRED AWAKE, THEN GROANED, feeling the hardwood floor beneath her. She rolled from her back to her side, aching slightly from the uncomfortable and fitful night of rest. She couldn't remember falling asleep, only that she awoke at some point in the night to see Althea still tending to Fable and Numair dozing in the armchair across the room.

Nora reached for Rowan, then bolted upright when she didn't feel him at her side. Her eyes scanned the oracle's cottage. The faint golden rays of morning filtered in through the windows. She glanced at the couch.

Fable was gone.

She jumped to her feet, then stopped when she heard a familiar sound—the sound of a dog lapping water from a bowl.

She strode from the living area into the kitchen to find Fable facing away from her, standing on shaky legs as he drank. Rowan stood watchful beside him.

Nora's throat closed as she took in the scene of her two dogs, side by side once more. Still facing away, Fable finished his drink and lifted his head. Streams of water dripped from his wet lips. A laugh caught in Nora's throat.

He'd always been a messy drinker.

The sound of her laughter drew Fable's attention. He turned.

Nora's heart skipped. "Fable," she whispered.

He limped over to her much quicker than he probably should have. Nora closed the distance and dropped to her knees before him.

"Oh, Fable." She drew him into a hug, and he pressed the top of his broad head against her chest, directly over her heart.

As he always had.

As if no time had passed.

As if *he* had never passed.

"Nora," he said softly.

She relished the sound of his voice, so different from Rowan's.

A patter of feet entered the kitchen behind her. Then someone cleared their throat.

"Good morning." Orella's voice.

Nora wiped a stray tear from her cheek, then turned to see the gray rabbit wearing a tiny woolen dress.

Keeping her voice to a whisper, Orella said, "Your friends arrived late last night with Arcturus."

Nora felt her shoulders drop in relief. "Is Cassian okay?"

Orella wiggled her pink nose, shifting her glasses. "He was very nearly frozen, but he should make a full recovery. Your Red friends took good care of him."

"Where are they?" Nora asked.

"In the loft, still sleeping."

"Numair and Althea?"

"They left before sunrise to get some rest and discuss some things with the other leaders of our village. They'll be back, though."

Nora shifted on her knees, then stood.

Orella glanced at Fable and Rowan. "The three of you need some time together. And Fable should get moving. A light walk would do him some good."

She crossed the kitchen to a tiny wooden table and lifted a satchel that sat on top of it.

"I've packed a hot breakfast for the three of you. Why don't you walk the beach, then come back when you're ready?"

Seeing her struggle with its weight, Nora took the satchel from the rabbit. "Ready for what?"

Orella waved her question away with a pink-padded paw. "Just come back when you're finished."

Nora looked down at Fable. "Are you sure he's well enough for a walk?"

"Why don't you ask him?"

Nora held his golden gaze, then said with a soft smile, "Fable? Do you want to go for a walk?"

His unmistakable answer came in the form of a swish of his fluffy tail.

Nora walked the pebbled beach with slow, measured steps. Fable hobbled along at her right side while Rowan trotted slightly ahead at her left. His dark-brown eyes scanned the terrain as if searching for danger. After several minutes, he finally seemed assured they were safe and slowed his pace to heel at Nora's side.

Gentle waves lapped the pebbled shoreline. Rowan walked with his feet in the water, and Nora wondered how his toes weren't frozen. The water had to be ice-cold. She cast a glance over her shoulder, noting how far they'd wandered from Orella's snowy lakeside cottage nestled between the dense pines.

"You doing okay?" she asked Fable.

"Yeah, it gets easier the more I move."

"Good," Nora said. "Good . . ." Her voice trailed off, full of questions.

The full blaze of morning light crested the mountains that surrounded them, glimmering off the water and illuminating the other tiny islands of Arcadia's archipelago. Smoke curled upward through the pines and into the frigid morning air, marking the locations of other cottages like Orella's.

Nora found a spot with a large flat rock and stopped to swing the satchel from her shoulders. Orella had provided a blanket, which Nora spread onto the cold stone, then began unpacking the breakfast: a canteen full of hot tea and a small clay dish containing a warm mash similar to porridge. When she found three wooden bowls inside the bag, she divided the food evenly, then took some from her own bowl and topped off Rowan's and Fable's.

She invited them to sit on the blanket and set the bowls before them. They stared at her, waiting for her to give them their cue. Fable drooled.

Nora grinned. "Take it," she said, as if she were serving up their regular dog food at home.

They dove in.

Rowan devoured his hungrily, tapping the white toes of his left hind foot with excitement as he ate. Even Fable ate faster than Nora expected. When they'd finished licking their bowls clean, she divided her untouched breakfast between them.

"Aren't you hungry?" Rowan asked.

"I'm okay," Nora said, unscrewing the lid from the canteen and sipping the tea. "Go ahead."

But she wasn't okay.

She watched Fable scarf down the second bowl of food, once again filled with a swell of mixed emotions that threatened to bubble to the surface and overflow.

The events of the past three days in Coeur caught up to her. Three days . . . or had it been years? Or seconds? According to Cassian, it could be anything with the time difference between realms.

The absurdity of it all clanged in her mind.

She kept waiting for this dream to come to an end.

For the moment she'd wake up and realize it was all a cruel nightmare and her dog would be stolen from her again.

Yet there he stood, sunlight outlining his body in a red-golden glow as he ate porridge.

He and Rowan switched bowls, just like they always did at home, and checked to make sure the other hadn't left any morsels.

When they'd finished, they settled onto the blanket with contented sighs. Fable's tongue flopped from the side of his mouth. Billows of condensation formed in front of him. He watched Nora with a curious expression before saying, "What?"

Tears stung her eyes. Heat filled her cheeks, and once again Nora's throat began to close. "How?" she breathed. "How are you here?"

He tilted his head to one side. "How am *I* here? Shouldn't you be asking how *you* are here?"

Fable's eyes looked brighter than when they'd left the cottage, his body more relaxed and at ease. He rolled onto his hip, still lying upright, and tucked one of his front paws beneath him, just like he always did.

Tears slipped from Nora's eyes and burned against her cold cheeks. She set the tea aside and clenched her hands in her lap as she gave words to the images that had haunted her the past several days.

"You died, Fable." Her voice cracked. "I watched you die. I held you as you died. I—We . . . we spread your ashes."

"Oh, Nora." Fable stood on shaky legs and closed the small distance between them. "I'm a little weak at the moment, but my strength will return. I am far from dead, Nora." Once again, he pressed the top of his head against her chest, allowing her to wrap her arms around him and bury her face against the back of his neck.

This time the dam that held Nora's tears burst. Shuddering sobs wracked her shoulders as she clutched Fable, pulling him closer.

Then closer.

As if she could draw him straight into her essence.

Straight into her heart.

"Don't you see?" Fable said.

"See what?" Nora sniffed and pulled back to look at him. Her eyes traced the familiar lines of his face: the deep creases of his forehead, the swirl of his button eyebrows, and the curve of his smile.

"I didn't die, Nora. But you *believed* I did," Fable said. "So, in a sense, you died, too, because you wanted to be with me."

She wiped her cheek.

"But I didn't die, Nora," he said. "I was reborn. And if you want to be with me, where I am, you must be reborn too."

CHAPTER THREE

BACK INSIDE THE COTTAGE, NORA FOUND Cassian seated on the floor beside the fire, a thick blanket draped around his shoulders. He clutched a bowl of porridge in one hand, a spoon in the other. He glanced up as she entered.

"Nora."

Before she could say anything, Eira and Taran crashed into her legs, their entire backsides wagging with joy.

"You're okay!" Eira said.

"Yes." Nora patted her head. "We're okay. But how are you guys?"

"Still cold," Cassian said as he stood. He crossed the room and stopped in front of her. "But very happy to see you alive and well." He reached down to pet Rowan and Fable. "You too, boys."

"Fable, this is Cassian," Nora said.

Cassian set his bowl on a side table and crouched before Fable. "I'm very glad to see you've recovered."

"It's nice to meet you, Cassian."

"You as well, Fable. It's clear you're a special Red to know." He glanced up at Nora. "I can tell."

She shifted from foot to foot, uncomfortable from his stare.

"As is Rowan," Cassian added when Nora's other dog wedged himself in between them. "The Eidolon of Coeur."

"Speaking of which . . ." Orella's voice drifted through the cottage as she moved from the kitchen to the living room, carrying a steaming bowl. "We have much to discuss regarding such things. So please, come have a seat."

Cassian touched Nora's arm as he stood. She followed him into the main room and found a seat on the couch where Fable had slept the night before. He and Rowan joined her, each taking a seat on either side of her.

Cassian returned to his spot by the hearth, blanket still draping his shoulders.

"Here, child." Orella thrust the bowl she'd been carrying into Nora's hands. More porridge. "Eat," Orella said. "You need your strength."

Nora started to ask how Orella knew she hadn't eaten yet, but the rabbit interrupted her, waving a paw through the air. "I'm an oracle, dear. I know things. Besides, I heard your stomach growl the moment you entered the cottage. Now eat."

Nora spooned a bite into her mouth. Flavors of cream, honey, and cinnamon melted onto her tongue. The porridge's warmth heated her from the inside, and soon, she found herself curling her legs beneath her as she scraped the bowl clean. She handed it to Orella when the rabbit offered to take it from her.

Feeling content with her full belly, Nora pulled her dogs closer and leaned back, feeling cozy enough to nap.

But a knock at the door interrupted that opportunity.

Eira and Taran trotted to the front door to see who'd arrived. Rowan and Fable didn't leave Nora's side but held their ears at attention, listening as

Orella opened the miniature door and greeted whoever stood outside.

"Wonderful timing," Orella said. "They're ready."

"Good."

Nora recognized Numair's feline voice from the porch.

"We have much to discuss," she said as she entered the cottage through the full-sized door. Althea heeled at her side.

Edric entered behind them, hooves clomping. He nodded in Nora's direction. Arcturus strode through the door next. His saffron eyes lit up when he saw her.

The click of another set of hooves announced the final guest. Nora stiffened when she saw the humanoid figure dip its head to fit a gigantic rack of antlers through the doorway—elk, if she wasn't mistaken. The man walked upright on long legs, hooves peeking out from beneath the hem of his woolen pants. But he wore no shirt. Instead, thick brown fur covered his broad shoulders and chest. She noted the mostly human face and how it contrasted with his oversized elk ears.

The five newcomers took their places around the living room. Arcturus lay on the floor, while Edric stood. Only Numair and the elk-man sat on the armchairs across from the couch. Althea curled up at Numair's feet.

Orella entered last, carrying a tray with tea and small carrot-shaped biscuits. She placed it on the coffee table in the center of the living room.

"Now that we're all gathered, allow me to make some introductions." She wiped her paws on the apron she wore over her dress, then removed it and set it aside. She crossed the room to a miniature rocking chair, identical to the one Finneas had in his cottage.

The oracle sat with a fatigued huff, removed her glasses, then perched them on top of her head. "Now where was I?" She glanced around the room. "Oh yes." She gestured with a paw in Nora's direction. "This is Nora, Rowan, and Fable. And their travel companions, Cassian, Eira, and Taran.

"Now, Nora, you've already met Arcturus." The sky lion dipped his head in greeting. "And Edric, one of our watchers here in Arcadia. And Numair of course." Orella pointed to the panther-woman. "She and her dog, Althea, serve on the Rebel council along with Edric and me. And this"—she paused, drawing her attention to the elk-man—"is the head of our council, Quince."

He bowed his head in greeting, and Nora found herself wondering how much his antlers weighed. They looked heavy. Spreading past his shoulders, they stretched as tall as they were wide.

"It's an honor to meet you, Nora," Quince said. "I'm sure you're wondering why we've all gathered."

Nora curled her fingers into her dogs' fur. "I'm guessing it has something to do with the Troves of Eylan. And Rowan, the"—she tried to remember the word—"the eidolon?"

Numair nodded. "Yes, and we're eager to hear the details of your journey." Numair shifted to the edge of her seat. Her hind paws peeked out from the hem of her tunic dress. She interlaced her fingers, balancing her elbows on her knees. "But first, *where* are you from? Clearly you're not from Coeur."

Nora started to answer, but Rowan interrupted. "We're from the Kingdom of Kentucky!" he said, then proceeded to tell them the story.

After he'd finished sharing the broad strokes of their journey, Nora filled in the details and answered their questions. Fable remained silent beside them, listening with rapt attention. His posture shifted when they got to the part about the first trove and the condition they'd found him in. Nora paused when his lips parted as if he wanted to speak.

"I still don't know how you ended up here," Nora said to him. "Or what exactly the queen did to you."

He cleared his throat and shifted from lying on the couch beside Nora to sitting. "A little over four weeks ago, I made my return to Coeur, passing from the Kingdom of Kentucky back into this realm."

Nora clenched her hands in her lap, listening as he spoke, noting the time difference between the realms. Fable had been in Coeur for weeks, but it had only been days since Nora last saw him. Though, she had to admit, it felt longer.

Much longer.

"Once I arrived, I knew I had to find my pack. And my mother, Princess Sadie."

"Sadie?" Nora asked.

He licked his lips and nodded.

"Wait, does that mean . . .?"

He nodded again, knowing her question before she spoke it. "I was one of the pups Sadie sent through the portal many years ago. Which is why I had to return."

Nora's mind spun as she recalled the moment she'd first met Fable, when she was five years old. The details were fuzzy, but she recalled the memory of walking through the aisles of the flea market with her father. One of the local farmers had a pen set up in front of his stall with three pudgy golden retriever pups. Nora had been so captivated by their adorable little faces, she'd only caught part of the conversation when the farmer explained to Nora's father how he'd found the pups in his barn. Of course Nora hadn't thought it out of the ordinary as she'd pleaded with her father to take one home.

"And Rowan . . ." Nora said, piecing together the stories from her childhood.

Three years later, she and her father had walked through the stalls of the flea market once more. This time, with Fable. Almost instinctively he'd led them back to that same shop with the same farmer, and once again the man had a pen full of puppies. Six this time. The farmer explained that he'd kept the one female pup from the first litter who'd now had puppies of her own.

"Sadie is Rowan's grandmother," Nora muttered under her breath.

Fable nodded while everyone else stared, waiting for them to conclude their private conversation.

"I knew I needed to find Sadie," Fable continued. "But Coeur looked different. I was so young when I was last here. I don't remember much beyond my den and the forest of pines in the hills of Yarou." He paused. "But during my return, I came upon a lost pup." A faraway look formed in Fable's eyes. "A Red. I knew he was one of Sadie's—my brother. He was running from a sky lion. I tried to save him, but . . ." Deep sorrow creased Fable's brow. "The sky lion got both of us."

Nora swallowed.

"I remember seeing the queen's castle," Fable said, "and the throne room. But the queen's subjects did something to me. I don't remember much after that. The pup . . . he looked near death when I last saw him."

Fable lowered his head.

"When I woke, I found myself in a very cold location, being placed into a large copper bowl on top of a pillar. It leeched the last ounces of energy from me, and I fell into a dark, dreamless sleep. Your face was the next thing I saw." He glanced up, placing his paw in Nora's hand. "I still wonder what she did to that pup. And where she took it."

His words tickled something in the back of Nora's mind. Princess Sadie had mentioned that one of her pups had gone missing.

"Arcturus," Nora said, directing her attention toward the sky lion. "You said when Queen Kierra captures a Red, she binds them to the troves to create a circuit."

He dipped his big head. "Eylan is a flowing force. When the Reds are connected to the troves, their Eylan is added to the stores, and their presence creates a current that maximizes the troves' power."

Quince cleared his throat. "Sorry to interrupt, but the details of your journey only confirm that it's time to move forward with our plan."

"What plan?" Nora asked, patting Fable's paw with a comforting stroke.

"Our plan to take the kingdom back from Queen Kierra," Quince said. "It's all coming together, just as the messenger said it would. Isn't that right, Orella?"

"It's true," the rabbit said. "Many years ago, a messenger visited me and two of the other oracles under the cover of night. It revealed one of the troves' locations to each of us and said only a whole human could undo Kierra's curse." She clasped her paws at her chest. Her eyes widened with wonder. "And here you are!"

Nora swallowed. "Finneas said there are three troves."

Orella nodded. "And each oracle knows of only one location."

"So you know where the next one is?"

"I do."

Nora draped her arms over Rowan and Fable and pulled them closer. "And I assume you want to send me there?"

"I do," Orella said. "If you are still willing."

Nora drew in a shaky breath, glanced at Rowan, feeling the Eylan Bond pulse between them. She looked to Fable next, still unable to believe he was truly alive. Once again, she had both of her dogs. She had everything she needed.

But that swelling, unsettling feeling returned in her gut: the fear of losing Fable again and the sickening sensation that this was all a dream.

That his presence wasn't real.

She couldn't allow him to be stolen from her again. And she couldn't allow something to happen to Rowan. She'd nearly lost him on Mount Croia.

Fear clenched her gut.

She had to protect them at any cost.

"Orella," Nora said as she exhaled, "it's time for me to take Rowan and Fable and go home."

The rabbit drew a sharp breath through her tiny nose.

Rowan and Fable stared at Nora as she spoke.

"Finneas said I could only return once I found the one who brought me here." She paused. "It was you, wasn't it? You're an oracle. You're part of the Rebellion. I don't blame you for bringing me here, but please . . . I need to go home. I must protect them." She glanced between Rowan and Fable.

Rowan's eyebrows pulled together. "But what about Coeur?" he asked. "You said we'd help the kingdom. We have to, Nora! They need us!"

"I said that before we knew how dangerous it would be. You almost died, Rowan."

He looked away, an expression of confusion and hurt on his face.

"We have your brother back," she said to him. "I won't allow something to happen to either one of you again."

Rowan refused to look at her.

Fable placed his paw on her leg. "Nora."

She turned to face him.

"I can't leave Coeur."

Her stomach dropped. "What?"

"And neither can you, I'm afraid," Orella said. "At least not yet. Because I didn't bring you here."

Nora slowly turned to face the rabbit. "What do you mean?"

Orella shrugged her tiny shoulders. "I don't know who brought you here, Nora. But it wasn't me. And Finneas is right. You can't leave until you find the one who summoned you through the portal."

"But what about Fable?" Nora asked. "Why can't he leave?"

"I don't fully understand the voyages between realms and portals," Fable said, "or the laws that govern them. But I passed from Coeur to Earth once long ago, knowing that one day, when the time was right, I would return." He paused. "Sometimes we're granted passage into another realm for a short season, sometimes for longer."

"So you can't leave . . . *ever*?"

"I didn't say that. I can't leave *now* just as you can't leave now. And since we *are* here now, we must *be* here now."

Cassian caught Nora's eye. Fable's words reminded her of something Finneas had said when they sat inside his cozy burrow in the highlands.

She glanced at Rowan seated on her other side, proudly wearing the aureus around his neck. She recalled his acts of bravery—rushing toward danger, not away from it. That's why he was an eidolon. Because he was willing to choose love over fear.

And wasn't that the very heart of the Eylan?

Nora swallowed, realizing that once again she had allowed fear to cloud her decisions.

But Rowan hadn't.

Rowan—that's the kind of character Nora wanted to have. She wanted to be a person who embodied the same strength she saw in her dog—the Eylan.

She thought back to the moment when Rowan clung to the planks of the broken bridge, remembered the trust and love she'd seen in his eyes. And though fear still clamored for her devotion, she shoved it aside and focused on the love she had for her dog—for both of her dogs—and the joy and gratitude of being reunited with Fable.

A log popped in the fire. The sound of gentle waves lapping at the pebbled beach sloshed outside the cottage.

"Coeur is Rowan's kingdom," Nora finally said. "Fable's too." She pressed her lips together, then declared, "So it shall be my kingdom as well. Coeur shall be my home."

Rowan nudged her hand.

"Because my home is with the two of you," she added, pulling Rowan and Fable even closer. "And if this is our home"—she faced Orella—"then we must take it back from the queen." She exhaled tensely. "That is the only way to protect them." She squeezed her dogs. "To protect Coeur."

Again she caught Cassian staring, his expression unreadable.

"And all the other realms," Rowan added.

"Right," Nora said, recalling Finneas's warning about Queen Kierra's intentions to spread her Bitter reign by creating portals to other worlds once she had enough power.

Numair cleared her throat. "A beautiful declaration, Nora, but you must know that this journey will only become more and more dangerous."

Nora nodded, mentally holding the fear at bay.

"The Reds have always been a target," Numair continued. "Rowan and Fable included. But now Rowan poses an even greater threat to the queen. He's an eidolon. There's now a bigger target on his back."

Nora swallowed.

"And . . ." Numair paused, glancing at Althea. "Do you want to tell her?" she asked her dog.

Althea stood from where she'd curled up beside Numair's feet. "While I was able to heal Fable, I was unable to restore his Eylan."

"What?" Nora asked.

"I'm not sure what the queen did to him," Althea said. "But if there is anything left of his power, it's completely undetectable."

"Fable, is this true?" Nora asked.

He lowered his head.

Nora cupped her hands around his face. "It's okay," she said quietly, so only he could hear. Then louder, she added, "All the more reason for me to be here. Can we get his Eylan back?"

Althea shook her head. "I don't know. I've never seen anything quite like it. He has no Bitter in his veins and no marks of any beast. I'm not sure what to make of it."

"It doesn't matter," Nora said. "I have Rowan. He and I are bonded." She winced as regret twinged in her gut. She draped an arm over Fable, wishing she had the same connection with him. "Fable may not have his Eylan, but Eira and Taran have theirs. And Cassian is great with a bow and arrow. We're ready." She stood. "We can leave for the next trove today."

Orella snorted a laugh. "You're most certainly not ready."

Arcturus shook his big lionlike head.

Nora scoffed. "What do you mean? You've been waiting for my arrival to come save your kingdom, and now you tell me I'm not ready?"

Numair gestured for Nora to sit down. "Arcturus told us he saw your attempts to wield the Eylan. He is"—she glanced at him—"concerned your skills are lacking."

The griffin stared at his talon-tipped paws, refusing to make eye contact.

Nora plopped back onto the couch. "But I unleashed the Eylan at the first trove."

"Rowan unleashed the Eylan," Numair clarified.

Nora pressed her lips together, then said, "Because of our bond."

"Yes, because of your bond. I'll give you that. You have access to tremendous power, Nora, but you have no control over it, no finesse. You must learn its subtleties if you're to outwit the queen at the next two troves and return all three aurei to the Great Mandala at the Temple of Eylan."

"No one said anything about returning the aurei to the temple."

Numair dipped her head. "You see. You're not ready. But we shall make you ready."

"How?"

"As an Eylan mystic, it was my responsibility to train those newly bonded and, after Queen Kierra's rampage, to prepare them to take back our kingdom." She stood, clasping her hands at her waist. "And I still bear that responsibility."

Quince leaned forward. "You will stay with us as long as possible within the safe confines of Arcadia," he said. "You and Rowan will train with Numair, and we will do our best to outfit you with everything you need for the next leg of your journey."

Numair's feline lips curled with a smile. "Rest up today, Nora. Your training starts tomorrow."

Thorne beat his wings against the air currents, flying east from the capital of Roone across the kingdom, his queen riding on his back. He'd carried countless hybrids during his months of training when he'd first joined the queen's court three years ago. All griffins practiced with saddles and riders, but Thorne never dreamed his training would lead to this moment and honor.

He gazed out at the lavender sky, seeing stars twinkle against the approaching night. Queen Kierra shifted in the saddle.

Though they'd been traveling for an entire day, she hadn't spoken a single word to him. He wondered if she'd soon suggest making camp for the night or if he'd need to broach the subject. It felt strange to think she might take orders from him on such a matter. Then again, if he found those Reds, he'd be delivering orders to an entire kingdom, an entire realm of his own. At least, that's what the queen had promised.

After Kierra had inducted him into her court, Thorne made it his business to learn his queen's objectives and his role in her pursuits. He, along with the other sects of chimeras, were to ensure the safety of the kingdom by removing all threats—the dogs, namely the Reds—and to recover the Eylan that rightfully belonged to the queen.

In the early days of Kierra's reign, several dog packs migrated south to the kingdoms of Smyredia and Valecrest, where they found refuge. Rumors spread about some of the dogs even crossing the sea to Iredorn, where they managed to seal off that kingdom as a realm through a portal. Upon hearing these rumors, the queen secured all borders to the neighboring kingdoms and announced the reward she'd bestow on the chimera who rid the land of every last Red—a laurel crown and an appointment as co-ruler once she'd expanded beyond their current realm.

From the moment Thorne learned of this prize, he knew he'd be the one to deliver.

"Griffin . . ." The queen spoke.

Thorne clenched his beak, wondering why she still didn't call him by his name.

"The air currents are quite strong," she said. "When do you expect us to reach Oorbara?"

Thorne relaxed his shoulders and tuned into his feathers, sensing the air. "At least three days, my crown."

"Three days?" She scoffed.

"At least three. Maybe longer. The warm currents are pushing northwest."

"Then drop south, straight across the lowlands. From there, we can fly due east. Once we cross into Oorbara, it should only take us a day to reach the nearest coast."

Us. Thorne reveled in the idea of being an *us* with his queen.

"*At least* a day," Thorne clarified. "The dunes of the eastern lands are vast."

"I am quite familiar with the terrain," she said tensely.

"Then you know it will take us some time to reach the sea. This is a long journey. We should begin searching for our camp for the night." Thorne filled his voice with confidence as he spoke.

"I also know that we've barely been in the air for twelve hours and griffins are trained to fly for at least double that. Darkness hasn't even fallen. Let's see if your eagle eyes are still worth their weight at night." She paused, a smile in her voice. "We fly straight through till morning. We'll make a short stop for provisions in the lowlands, and then we won't stop again until we reach the edge of Oorbara. From there, it will only take us a day to reach the coast. Is that understood?"

Thorne beat his wings in frustration. During his training he'd learned to keep up with even the most grueling of flight schedules. He could easily fly all night. But what he couldn't bear was the idea of his time with the queen cut short. This was his moment after all—his moment to prove himself as her champion.

Then again, the sooner they reached Oorbara, the sooner he could serve Kierra in whatever other capacities she needed.

Feeling emboldened by this idea, he dared to ask, "Why Oorbara, my crown? What do you expect to find in the most eastern parts of our kingdom?"

"Nothing that concerns you, Thorne," she said. "Now fly. Don't waste another drop of your energy with questions. Just get us to the Sea of Oorbara as quickly as possible."

The sound of his name on her lips brought a curled smile to his beak. "Yes, my crown," he said and shifted their flight path due south.

CHAPTER FOUR

NORA SPUN, TAKING IN THE SURROUNDINGS of the circular clearing where she stood. Giant boulders sat at odd intervals along the perimeter intermingled with makeshift gym equipment constructed from pine boughs and stones. Beneath her booted feet, fine-eroded pebbles from the beach coated the ground with a texture similar to sand. This, Numair had told her, was the training island.

Nora peered up, watching as Arcturus soared through the sky, returning to the larger island where Orella lived to retrieve the others, who would soon join Nora on the smaller Arcadian landmass.

She sucked in a deep breath of the crisp air while she waited, admiring the towering ring of evergreens that formed the arena's boundary and the Arcadian mountains beyond that shimmered a silvery lavender in the midmorning light. Waves lapped the frigid shore in the distance.

The flight over had provided a breathtaking view of Arcadia. In the light of day, Nora had seen dozens of cottages through the trees on each of the small islands, even a town square in the middle of the largest landmass. She'd watched in awe over Arcturus's shoulder as he'd swooped low, granting her view as chimeras of all shapes and sizes began their day. The sleepy village quickly came alive with music and laughter. A palpable joy had lifted from the town square, rising through the atmosphere as Arcturus had flown her from one island to the next.

Nora wiped her clammy palms on her woolen pants, feeling nervous. She adjusted the matching tunic, both given to her by Numair. Cassian, who'd ridden over with Eira and Taran, sat on one of the boulders across the clearing, also in borrowed but clean clothes.

Eira and Taran paced the circle, sniffing every rock and leaf, while Rowan and Fable sat at Nora's heels, waiting for Numair, Althea, and Orella to show up.

"Are you nervous?" Fable asked, nudging her leg with his nose.

She reached down and rested her hand on top of his broad head, then curled her fingers behind his ear to ruffle his feathery-soft fur. Every time she touched him, every time she peered into his golden eyes, she felt as if she were stepping back in time, into a memory, into something that wasn't real.

But he *was* real.

As real as Rowan.

She knelt between her dogs and pulled them closer. "I'm terrified," she said. "But I'll do anything to be with both of you." She scratched under their chins. "This kingdom is home to all of us now. I'll do everything in my power to protect it—to protect you."

They licked her hands.

"I wish you still had your Eylan," Nora said to Fable as she ruffled the fur on his chest.

He nudged her hand. "I have you."

A large shadow crossed the clearing.

Nora kissed the top of Fable's head, then Rowan's, then stood.

Arcturus landed at the far edge of the clearing, delivering Numair, Althea, and Orella.

The panther-woman stalked across the circle toward Nora. Sunlight glinted on her silky, black skin and fur. "My, it feels like ages since I last stood in this arena," she said, glancing around.

Orella hopped on all fours to keep up with Althea as they joined them. "And I've not flown in nearly as long," she said. "I forgot how horrifying it is." She stopped to scratch her ear with her long hind foot. It was the most rabbitlike thing Nora had seen her do. The oracle noted Cassian across the clearing. "I think I'll join the boy until my head stops spinning." She shot a glare at Arcturus. "You could have taken those turns a little easier."

Nora fought back a smile as she watched the griffin smirk, then leap into the sky to return to the main island.

Numair cleared her throat, drawing Nora's attention as she interlaced her long fingers and dropped her hands to her waist. Nora noted the unusually long—and sharp—nails that tipped the woman's human appendages.

"And so we begin," Numair said, raising a dark eyebrow. "The first part of your training is to recognize the power you have access to. You must respect this power if you're to use it for good. Do you understand?"

"Yes," Nora replied.

"No," Numair said in a stern tone.

Nora stiffened.

"No, you do not understand. But you will." Numair stroked the top of Althea's head. "When you're bonded to a Red, you're given access to a great gift. The Reds have more Eylan than any other creature because of their purity of heart."

Nora reached down and touched her own dogs. "That I understand," she said.

Numair nodded. "I'm sure you do. And because you're bonded to an eidolon, that power is even greater. But I'm not sure you understand just how rare this gift is. This is the *only* way for a human to access the power of an aureus. Because of your bond with Rowan, you have a direct channel to the wellspring of Eylan. To be a conduit of this power, an extension of the Red you're bonded to, you must become as open and pure of heart as they are. You can't allow low emotions to weigh down the bond."

"Like fear," Nora said, recalling her experience at Mount Croia.

"Yes, fear is the lowest," Numair said. "But there are other emotions that can disrupt the bond as well. Emotions are energy in motion. Every emotion has a vibration to it. And it affects the bond and the flow of Eylan in unique ways."

"Love?" Nora asked. "Is that the highest?"

"Correct. *Pure* love. *Unconditional* love. A love free of conditions like fear, anxiety, frustration, or rage. It's not as common or as easy to wield as you might think." Numair paused. Her yellow panther eyes scrutinized Nora's face. "Though I think you understand that as well."

Nora glanced away, trying to block the image of Rowan dangling in the gray sky, hanging by a thin glowing thread. "I understand," she said in a quiet voice.

"Good." Numair strolled to the very center of the clearing.

"Since each emotion has a vibrational speed, that emotion controls the speed at which Eylan flows through the bond. If it flows at all. It can become completely blocked if the vibration is too low."

Nora followed and stood beside her.

"Now, I'd like you to begin by tapping into your bond with Rowan to make it visible."

Nora sucked in a deep breath. "Okay," she said as she called him to her with a gesture.

Rowan eagerly sprinted the short distance.

Fable waited where he sat.

Nora knelt in front of Rowan and placed her hands on his shoulders.

"I'm ready!" he said, body trembling with excitement.

Nora smiled, then leaned her forehead against his. She closed her eyes, feeling his warmth, listening for the sound of his breath.

She moved one of her hands to cover his chest and waited until she could feel the pulse of life within him. Then she covered her own heart with the other hand.

She breathed his name. "Rowan."

Energy alighted in her chest and shot down her left arm. When she opened her eyes, a thick cord of liquid-light shone between them.

"Well done," Numair said.

Nora stood and watched the cord stretch between her and Rowan. She glanced at Fable. Longing washed over her as she caught his stare. Though he'd been returned to her, she still felt disconnected from him. She blinked, sucked in a deep breath, then faced Numair. "Now what?"

"Now we start with the basics."

Numair motioned for Eira and Taran to join them in the center. Cassian and Orella remained seated on the boulder, warming themselves in the sun.

"Wielding the Eylan is as instinctual to a Red as breathing," Numair said. "So although Rowan didn't grow up here in Coeur, you should trust his abilities. *Always* trust him," she said with emphasis. "If for no other reason than the fact that trust has a much higher vibration than doubt and will keep your bond strong in times of great trouble."

"Got it," Nora said.

"You should also trust him because he'll likely always be right. Reds are far wiser than humans. And much more attuned to the energetic tapestry of the universe."

Nora thought of the "sixth sense" people often mentioned when talking about dogs. It suddenly made more sense.

She patted Rowan's head. "I promise to always trust you."

His tail swished along the ground as he peered up at her with a smile.

"The next thing you should know," Numair continued, "is that each Red has a base power that's connected to one of the elements or forces of the universe."

"I don't understand," Nora said.

Numair nodded knowingly. "Taran?"

"My elemental power is storm!" He barked, and thunder crackled.

Nora's eyes widened. "The lightning!"

He barked again, sending a flicker across the sky.

Nora turned to Eira. "So your power must be snow, right?"

"Close," Eira said, licking Nora's hand. "My power is water—in all of its forms."

Excited, Nora faced Rowan. "What's yours?" she asked, thinking of the bubble he'd wrapped her in to protect her from the fish chimera.

"I don't know," he said, looking to Numair. "It felt instinctual to wield it, just like you said. But I don't know what it is."

The panther-woman shrugged and looked to Eira and Taran for an answer. "You've seen him wield. Do you know?"

The two Reds exchanged a glance, paused, then Taran said, "Air, I think."

Eira nodded but looked uncertain.

Numair narrowed her eyes, then said, "Very well. Air." She wore an odd expression.

"Is that good?" Rowan asked. His button eyebrows pulled together with concern.

"Oh yes. They're all good—all powerful. I suspect their hesitation comes from the fact that air is often confused with another element, an arcane element called *ether*. But never mind that for now." Numair faced Nora. "When you're bonded to a Red, you have access to their base power—their element. And when you wield it, that power will blend with your own innate spark of Eylan that all humans have—well, *had*." She and Cassian caught each other's eye across the arena.

"The Eylan that flows in every being is the same and also unique. It's the same because it comes from the same source—the Genesis. But it's also as unique as the person or animal who bears it. Bonds are typically formed because there's a common or shared identifying marker the dog and human recognize in one another—a common thread in the great tapestry of the Eylan. You're drawn to one another because you recognize that what is in you is also in him." Numair pointed to Rowan. "This commonality is the basis of a bond and is what allows you to have access to his elemental power, in this case"—she paused—"air."

Nora nodded. "Got it."

"Now, clearly you've wielded the Eylan."

"Yes."

"How did you manifest it?"

Nora thought for a moment. "It was like a pulse. A blast of air. I guess that makes sense for Rowan's—" She paused, recalling the term. "His elemental power."

"Right," Numair said, her tail flickering behind her. Her eyes slid to Taran and Eira, but she directed her words at Nora. "So let's see you wield, then."

"Right now?"

Numair's panther ears twitched. "Yes. Now."

Nora cleared her throat and backed up a step, gathering herself.

"Do you see that target?" Numair pointed across the clearing to what looked like an archery bull's-eye suspended on two strings from a rectangular pine structure. It hung heavy and immovable in the gentle breeze.

"Yes," Nora said.

"I want you to hit it."

"Hit it?"

"Like you did with the chimera on the mountainside," Eira said. "Like you did with the beast at the trove. Hit it with your pulse."

Nora shifted from foot to foot. "Okay, I'll try."

Numair's eyes slitted in scrutiny.

"What?"

"Nothing," the panther-woman said. "Go on."

Nora patted her thigh, and Rowan pressed himself against her, whining with excitement. She peered down at the glowing bond between them and focused her attention on the flickers of light that flowed through the liquid-like connection. It appeared thinner than the last time she'd seen it. Or was it?

She chewed her bottom lip, sucked in a deep breath, then raised her hands.

She felt silly. Ridiculous, in fact.

Everyone locked eyes on her, but Cassian's stare made her the most uncomfortable.

She tried to shift her focus to the sensation of the bond, the vibration of energy that wrapped around her wrist. She could barely feel the tingle in her left arm. Nothing in her right. She focused on its absence, trying to force a sensation of connection where there was none. Nerves twisted her gut. She swallowed, as if it would keep the butterflies from fluttering up her throat and out of her mouth, exposing her as the fraud she knew she was.

Who was she to save a kingdom?

"Well?" Numair said.

The sound of the panther-woman's voice jolted Nora from her thoughts. She startled and shoved her hands straight out in front of her.

As with the fish chimera in the gulch, nothing happened.

The target didn't so much as flutter.

Heat flushed Nora's cheeks when she saw Cassian's disappointed gaze slide away from hers.

Orella, who sat beside him, let out a soft sigh.

Rowan nudged her hand as if to say it was okay, that she'd get it the next time. Frustrated, Nora yanked her hand away.

A hurt look lingered on Rowan's face, and the cord of their bond thinned.

"I don't understand why sometimes it works and sometimes it doesn't," she huffed.

"Yes, you do," Taran said, then gnawed on a stick he'd found.

Nora clenched her teeth, irritated at his assumption. "No, I don't."

"Yes, you do," Eira said, dropping into a playful bow before Taran. She snatched the stick from him, then took off running.

Nora folded her arms over her chest, then turned back to Numair. "The emotional vibration?"

Numair merely dipped her head.

Rowan quivered beside her, restraining himself from running with his friends.

"But I'm not afraid right now." Nora's body tensed as she protested. "So why isn't it working?"

"Because as I said, *all* emotions affect the bond." Numair circled her. "And mainly because you were *trying*."

Nora furrowed her brow.

"Your intention matters. I've already defined emotions for you. What are they?"

Nora thought for a moment. "Emotion is energy in motion."

Numair nodded. "Yes. And when you *try* to do something there is an intention of struggle, something that requires force. Eylan cannot be forced. It flows." She reached down and scooped up a handful of the tiny pebbles, then allowed them to slip through her fingers. "Fear is one of the emotions the body feels. But not all emotions feel the same. So what did you feel when I asked you to wield?"

"I don't know."

Numair crossed her arms and waited.

Nora sighed, then thought for another moment. Her eyes caught Cassian's. Softly she said, "Nervous."

Numair tilted her head. "Nervous. Good. What else?"

"I don't know, maybe embarrassed to have everyone staring at me. It feels like a lot of pressure."

"Yes, well it is a lot of pressure. This is no small thing we've asked you to do: to battle chimeras, unleash the Troves of Eylan, and save the Kingdom of Coeur from the curse of Queen Kierra."

"Not helping," Nora said.

Numair ignored her and instead asked, "What else did you feel?"

When Nora didn't answer, Numair said, "Uncertain, perhaps? Uncertain that you could wield again? And on command?"

Nora nodded. "Incapable."

"Aha!" Numair snapped. "Powerlessness, precisely. And that's about as low of a vibration as you can have. Practically no vibration at all. Which is why I suspected you'd fail this challenge."

Nora jerked her head back, feeling slapped by Numair's words. "Because you knew I was powerless?"

Numair's whiskers pulled to the side as she smiled. "No, because I knew you *felt* powerless."

"How did you know that? I didn't even know that until a second ago."

"Because when you *try* to do something, it assumes a lack of power. Those who *know* they have the power don't *try*. They *do*. They *flow*."

Her words tickled Nora's mind.

"You have the power, Nora. Isn't that right, Eira?"

Across the clearing, Eira froze. She gripped one end of the stick while Taran tugged at the other. "It's true," she said through clenched teeth. "I've seen it."

Taran growled his agreement.

Rowan nudged her hand again. "I've seen it too! I can see it right now." His dark-brown eyes fixated on the cord of their bond.

"Rowan is a Red," Numair said. "He has innate power. And he's also an eidolon, bonded to the Eylan in an even more powerful way. And you are bonded to him. You are not powerless. You are powerful."

As Numair spoke, the cord of Eylan between Nora and Rowan hummed, thickening.

"Now, let's go again," Numair said.

Nora raised her hands.

"Don't think. Just flow."

"Don't think. Just flow," Nora repeated.

She pushed her hands forward, not forcing anything. A gentle pulsing sensation bumped her palms. The target across the clearing remained still, then fluttered.

"Yes!" Numair said with more enthusiasm than Nora thought the piddly action deserved.

"I hardly moved it."

"That doesn't matter. What matters is that you *did* move it. Because you do have the power. Think of it like this." Numair lowered her voice to a whisper. "When I talk like this, you can barely hear me, right?"

"Right," Nora said, unintentionally lowering her volume to match Numair's.

"But I do have a voice. I *can* speak."

Her words made Nora instinctively look to Rowan, then Fable.

"If I want to be heard more clearly"—Numair's voice had risen to a normal speaking volume—"and by more people"—she'd raised it again—"all I have to do is increase my volume!" She was shouting by the end of it. She chuckled to herself. "Or think of it this way: If you have a large body of water, say a river, that is blocked by a dam, the water doesn't flow. But it's still there. If a crack forms in the dam, the water trickles through. To release the full power and potential of that river, you don't need to force it through the crack; you must simply break open the dam. All you must do is let go of that which stands in the way. It is not about force. It is about letting go."

Her words sat heavy in Nora's mind. She glanced back at Fable.

"Now, go again."

Nora sucked in a deep breath, closed her eyes, and raised her hands. A picture of the Hoover Dam formed in her mind. She'd seen it on a trip she'd taken with her parents out west. She pictured the Colorado River and the massive wall that held it back, then imagined what would happen if a crack were to form in that wall. She saw the trickle of water in her mind's eye. A jagged line, darkening the stone of the dam. Water sputtered. Then gushed. A geyser erupted as the crack widened beneath the pressure of the river.

A jolt of energy fired from Nora's chest, raced down both her arms, into her hands, then left her palms.

Her eyes flew open in time to see ripples of liquid-light leave her hands and crash into the target. It swung backward as if someone had smashed it with a mallet.

Orella cheered and hopped up and down on the boulder beside Cassian. A contagious grin spread across his face.

"You did it!" Rowan shouted, then licked Nora's hand. Fable rushed to join her, nearly knocking her over. She grinned to see him alive with so much energy.

"I did it," Nora said, relieved.

Numair's yellow eyes remained fixed on the target. It swung back and forth until it slowly came to rest. She exchanged glances with Eira and Taran before facing Nora.

"Yes, you did it. But you'll need to be able to do much more than move a target if you're to defeat the queen. Come," she said, motioning for Nora to follow. "There is still much more for you to learn."

CHAPTER FIVE

NUMAIR LED NORA THROUGH THE PINES toward the water's edge on the small training island. She held out her left hand as she walked and drew a downward spiral with her finger through the air.

"Always remember that low-vibrating emotions have a tendency to spiral into *even lower* energies, pulling you downward until they completely block the flow of Eylan through your bond."

Nora nodded as she listened, recalling her experiences with fear on Mount Croia.

Numair stopped when she reached the water's edge. Nora joined her, seeing the larger island where Orella lived across the lake.

"Next lesson," Numair said as Rowan and Fable came to sit at Nora's side. Cassian, Eira, Taran, and Orella watched from a distance.

"One of the greatest challenges, and perhaps the only real challenge, of wielding is that you must learn to control the flow of your energy. Most people and creatures live outward to inward, meaning they allow their environment to influence their energy and their emotions. As a wielder, you must learn to live inward to outward, which is to say you control your inner environment, which then allows you to influence the environment around you."

"I'm not sure I understand," Nora said.

Numair dipped her head. "It's quite windy on the water today, is it not?"

Nora pushed the loose strands of hair from her face. "Yes."

"What if I told you that you could stop the wind? Or command its currents at your will? To create waves or still them by the movement of air?"

Nora's eyes widened.

Numair raised her eyebrows. "Rowan?"

He jumped to all fours. "Yes!" he said, tail swishing.

"Command the wind to cease."

Without hesitation, without an ounce of question or uncertainty, Rowan shouted, "Stay, Wind!"

Immediately, the gusts vanished. The waves relaxed to a gentle slosh. Even the pines on the island ceased to sway.

"Incredible," Nora breathed, feeling a ripple of power through the visible bond.

"You can do it too," Numair said. "Command it to return."

Filled with wonder at what she'd just seen her dog do, Nora said, "Wind, come!"

A violent gust nearly knocked her off her feet. Nora burst with laughter, and Orella cheered. Cassian grinned broadly, though his chilled expression suggested he preferred the wind to *stay* rather than *come*.

"That was awesome!" Nora said over the gale.

Fable nudged her hand. "Good job, Nora!"

"Well done," Numair said. "Now, command it to stop."

"Stay, Wind," Nora said calmly, a soft smile on her lips.

As it had moments ago, the wind died down until the air was completely still. The beach warmed a degree or two in its absence.

"You're becoming more confident," Numair said. "That's good. Confidence will pull your vibration higher."

Nora grinned. "Maybe I can do this."

"You can!" Rowan said, bumping her thigh with his nose. "*We* can!"

Nora scratched his head. "Yes, *we* can."

A sly grin spread across Numair's whiskered face. "Next lesson?"

"Sure," Nora said, excitement building.

"Very well. As I said, the real challenge is to maintain control of your energetical movement—your Eylan's current—even when the environment is not in your favor. That could be the physical environment of nature—say a storm."

Nora glanced at Taran.

"It could be the behaviors of others—say an attack from a griffin or other chimeras in service to the queen. Or it could be other difficulties and painful circumstances—such as the death of a loved one."

Nora's smile faded. She swallowed, her throat suddenly feeling tight.

"The journey ahead is dangerous, Nora."

Nora pressed her lips together. "More dangerous than facing a polar bear chimera or crossing a fraying rope bridge?"

"Much more dangerous," Numair said. "Which is why you must learn to control your internal environment. You can't control the outer environment, only influence it."

Nora reached down and touched Fable and Rowan.

"Are you ready to put your abilities to the test?"

Nora glanced at Cassian, who stood in a patch of sunlight, arms wrapped around himself. Orella huddled at his feet, looking nervous.

"I suppose I don't have a choice," Nora said, feeling a flicker of nerves. "What do I need to do?"

"Swim," Numair commanded.

"Excuse me?"

Numair raised her eyebrows. "I said *swim*."

"But I'll freeze," Nora protested.

"You've been cold before," Numair said.

"Yes, but cold water is different. I could develop hypothermia."

Numair shook her head. "You won't. Trust me. More importantly, trust Rowan."

Nora hesitated, then obeyed, stripping down until she stood only in her base layers: a long-sleeved undershirt and thick pair of leggings. She removed her socks last, placing her bare feet on the cold pebbles of the beach. Swallowing her nerves, she stepped into the water, then sucked in a sharp breath through gritted teeth.

"Go on," Numair encouraged.

The water encircled Nora's ankles, her calves, then her thighs.

"Keep going."

When the water hit her belly, Nora gasped. "Is this good?" she asked in a tight voice.

"All the way out," Numair commanded. "Till you can't touch."

Nora glanced at her dogs, who watched from the shore without a hint of concern.

By the time the water encircled Nora's neck, an uncontrollable shiver had worked its way through her body and rippled the visible golden bond between her and Rowan.

Numair turned to face him. "Rowan, command the wind."

Nora locked eyes with her dog from where she bobbed in the water.

He blinked, then said to Numair, "But she doesn't want me to."

"But she does want to learn," Numair replied.

Rowan's eyes shifted from Numair to Nora, then back again.

"You won't hurt Nora," Numair said. "You would never hurt her."

"Never," Rowan said emphatically.

"She is in no real danger."

"I know," he said.

"It's okay, Rowan," Nora called to him, teeth chattering. "Go on."

"Wind," Rowan said, "come!"

An icy blast of air whipped Nora's face. She kicked her legs to keep afloat. Without warning, a giant wave pummeled her from behind, pulling her under. Nora tumbled beneath the frigid waves. An instinct to gasp at the cold threatened to pull the icy water into her lungs, but she resisted and instead kicked for the surface.

Her head broke the water, but she could no longer control the full-body shivers.

"Breathe!" Numair commanded.

Nora sucked air too rapidly. A lightheaded feeling washed over her with a hint of panic.

She couldn't think past the cold.

Her bond thinned.

"Rowan," Numair said, "command the wind to move faster."

Nora barely heard his voice as another violent wave towed her under.

Her bare feet hit the smooth stones of the bottom, and she pushed upward.

"Nora!" Numair called to her. "Command the wind to stop."

Nora squeezed her eyes closed and tried to force her lips to move, but they wouldn't.

Her muscles locked up. Tremors ripped through her arms and legs as her body instinctually tried to warm itself.

Between the crashes of the waves and the howl of the wind, Nora heard Numair tell Rowan to command the wind to blow harder.

The current shifted and pulled Nora farther out into the lake, the water churning as violently as a tropical storm.

But there was nothing tropical about the temperature.

Her bond with Rowan winked in and out.

Nora couldn't feel her toes, her fingers.

An icy loneliness settled over her and unlocked something inside her at a cellular level.

Hot tears streaked down her cheeks as the grief that had been stored in her body cracked and splintered like ice, shattering her insides.

Powerlessness didn't even begin to describe the emotion Nora felt as the cold stole her ability to think, to move. She couldn't even see the shore or her dogs anymore.

Or her bond with Rowan.

How could she control the current of Eylan if she couldn't control the tremors in her own body? How could she protect Rowan and Fable if she couldn't overcome the frigid waters of Arcadia? And how could she save the Kingdom of Coeur if she couldn't rise above the frozen waves to tell the winds to cease?

She gasped, accidentally taking in water. She sputtered and coughed, causing her lungs, then her entire body, to spasm.

Another wave pulled her under, but this time, the undertow caught her, pulling her straight down.

Panicking, Nora grasped with her hands at the water. She kicked her legs but couldn't reverse the movement of her body.

Her frozen muscles finally ceased their shivering, now too tensed and locked up. A stillness enveloped her as she sank deeper, then deeper into the darkness of the lake.

The water burned her skin with its icy embrace. Her lungs spasmed for a breath.

She couldn't move her frozen limbs, and even if she could, the surface was too far away.

As she sank even deeper, Nora thought of the downward spiral Numair had drawn through the air with her finger as she described the descending vortex of low-vibrating emotions.

Down, down, down, they pulled.

Just like the lake.

Nora suppressed another lung spasm, squeezing her eyes closed against the coldness, the darkness, the nothingness.

In seconds, she'd pass the point of controlling the instinctual gasp of her lungs.

She searched her memory for Numair's instruction, but her thoughts felt as frozen as her body.

Another spasm.

Then another.

I'm dying, she heard her own voice say in her head. She yielded to the thought.

But then another voice broke into her mind.

Fable's.

His words from their first morning in Arcadia returned to her as clearly as if he were speaking them into her ear, as if he descended beneath the waves with her.

"*I didn't die, Nora. But you believed I did,*" Fable had said. "*So, in a sense, you died, too, because you wanted to be with me. But I didn't die, Nora. I was reborn. And if you want to be with me, where I am, you must be reborn too.*"

Nora's lungs spasmed again.

And this time, she gasped.

Her lips parted, lungs pulled, filling themselves with . . .

Air.

Nora's eyes shot open. A glowing bubble surrounded her head, filled with oxygen-rich air.

"Rowan," Nora's shivering lips whispered into the protective bubble he'd sent to her.

She kicked for the surface, breathing air inside the bubble of liquid-light.

Her head crested the surface. The bubble of Eylan burst as if it were made of nothing more than soapy suds.

The winds and waves still raged, but a voice reached her. An audible voice this time, as if sent to her on a gentle breeze.

"Nora." Rowan's voice kissed her ear. "I'm here," he said, though she knew he was still far away on the shore.

He was with her, though.

They were bonded to each other.

The thought alone sparked a flare of gratitude in her chest. The golden thread between them became visible once more, re-tethering her to the dog she loved. She imagined Fable sitting beside him and once again felt overwhelmed with longing, wishing to be bonded to him in the same way she was bonded to Rowan.

"Nora?"

Fable's voice this time. As if Rowan had sensed her emotions through the bond and sent a message from Fable on the breeze.

"I'm here," Fable said. "We're both here. We haven't left you. And you haven't left us. You can do this, Nora."

She fought back tears as an overwhelming wave of gratitude washed over her.

And suddenly, she understood what she had to do.

"I must learn to control the flow of my energy," Nora said through chattering teeth as she treaded water. "Most people live outward to inward. I must learn to live inward to outward by controlling my inner environment." Nora wondered if Rowan could hear her on the wind or simply feel her through the bond. "Emotion is energy in motion. All I have to do is change the direction of my energy."

The bond visibly thickened, filling her with hope, which in turn thickened the bond even more. She could feel the energy begin to flow, flooding her body with a humming warmth. "When I start to sink, all I have to do is swim up." She smiled, now understanding why her gratitude had saved Rowan on Mount Croia.

"Thank you, Rowan," she said. "Thank you for saving me."

"You were always safe." She heard his reply in the wind, and her gratitude swelled.

Energy surged in Nora's chest, pulsed down her arms, her legs, banishing the cold from her body, the ice from her veins. And even though she could still feel the cold, it did not touch her. And though the waves and winds still raged, they did not sweep her under.

Lifting her face to the sky, Nora shouted, "Wind, stay!"

And immediately it obeyed.

CHAPTER SIX

Q UEEN KIERRA STOOD ON THE SANDY shores that kissed the Sea of Oorbara. The griffin, Thorne, stood behind her, watching with a scrutinizing avian gaze. His eagle eyes narrowed, the yellow irises contracting around perfectly round pupils. Kierra had never grown accustomed to the griffins' penetrating stares, nor the predatory way they cocked their heads.

The chimera's giant talons sank into the sand as it approached. She held up a hand to keep him at a distance.

Kierra hobbled a few steps closer to the water's edge, her already cumbersome gait made more difficult after riding in the saddle of a griffin for three days. It had been worth it, though, to push the creature and herself to the brink of exhaustion. They'd shaved an entire day off their travel time. And every minute counted when her power stood at risk of being seized. Every second they delayed was another opportunity for the whole human and the Reds to advance upon her kingdom. Already Kierra could feel the waning connection to her energy stores. She knew the trove at Mount Croia had been compromised, felt the instant her power had been leeched. Which meant the girl would go to one of two locations next.

Kierra knew which one was the most likely. And she'd stop her long before she ever reached it.

Kierra stared out at the open sea where clear skies reigned over the sapphire waters. The midday heat radiated off the sand and washed over her, pushed by a sea breeze. A strange energy tingled in the air. Ripples of Eylan. Faint but detectable.

Kierra cursed under her breath.

She'd been right.

How those blasted Reds had managed to undermine her plan she'd never know. But she wouldn't allow them to succeed. Not when she'd worked this hard and come this far to protect him.

"Makk . . ." She spoke his name into the wind, grateful to know he was safely back at the castle under the watchful eyes of hundreds of griffins and other chimerical soldiers who served in her court.

Still, she felt anxious in his absence. She always did. Which was why she never let him out of her sight, away from her protective presence. Unless it was absolutely necessary.

Not since the early days of her reign had she left him alone for this long. Since then, she'd always sent her most trusted warriors to do her bidding— then fed them to the ammit once they'd returned, ensuring her secrets died along with them.

She hadn't offered it a meal in five weeks, not since the last two griffins she'd sent to the troves to imprison her newly obtained Reds.

The monster would be ravenous when she returned.

Kierra shuddered at the mental image of that deranged amalgamation with the maw of a crocodile, the mane and prowess of a lion, and the crushing girth of a hippopotamus. She'd feed the ammit every last creature in Coeur if it meant protecting her beloved Makk. She wouldn't allow anything to happen to him.

Not again.

Against her will, images from the scene of his death drifted through her mind. The energetic vibration of each memory pulsed through her Bitter blood.

She'd found Makk when he was just a puppy and she just a girl, living on the streets of Coeur. Her mother, a drunk, and her absent father had left her no choice but to live as an orphan, begging for bread. In a dark alley one day, while digging through dumpsters behind a bakery in the village, she'd found the pink-bellied little Red hiding in a stack of trash. He came straight to her with no fear and licked her dirty face. And from that moment on, Makk was her dog, loyal till the end.

She tried to shut out the images of that day, when as a teenager she'd been dozing under the bridge where she and Makk slept, seeking shade from the oppressive summer heat. Startled from her nap, Kierra awoke to see three young men approaching with evil intentions in their eyes.

They attacked.

She screamed.

But no human came to her rescue.

Only Makk.

He wielded a magical force she'd only heard of in legends and stories.

But the three men overpowered him.

They killed him.

In the wake of Makk's death, a tremendous amount of power surged into Kierra's body and mingled with her grief, her rage, her fury.

The men ran from her presence. They got away that day, but they were not so lucky a year later when she found them on the outskirts of the village.

Left alone under the bridge with the cooling body of her dog, Kierra's insides swelled and writhed with wrath, mingled with an aching grief, and spiraled into a whirlpool of desolation.

She couldn't explain what happened next. Even now, the memories felt foggy.

Beside the gurgling brook beneath the bridge, she wept bitter, empty tears, begging Makk to return to her, to not leave her all alone.

The more she pleaded, the more the roiling power surged in her veins, clouding her vision, filling her mind with a darkness that blinded her to anything but her dead dog lying in the mud in front of her. That's when she saw the snake. A small, nonpoisonous water serpent sunning itself on a rock. She'd killed snakes before. Eaten them when she'd had to. But only out of necessity. But this time the hunger that drove her was something far deeper than physical hunger. The emptiness hollower than her empty belly.

She smashed the snake with a rock, feeling a jolt of dark power. She turned to walk away from it, but an opportunist hawk came to seize the serpent for its lunch.

She couldn't remember what happened after that. The next memory she had was of herself crouched over Makk's dead body with the lifeless hawk and snake beside him as her mumbling lips chanted words she didn't understand.

Tendrils of a viscous, black, shimmery substance streamed from her fingertips, swirling and coalescing in front of her. The black threads entered the serpent, then the hawk, then her dog.

Thick, dark vaporous clouds rolled across the ground, blanketing the scene in an impenetrable haze. When the darkness finally dispersed, Makk still lay before her, the bodies of the serpent and hawk gone. He sat up with a start, blinking at Kierra with familiar eyes. But hardly any other part of him looked the same.

Shock had jolted through Kierra's veins. For less than a second, she wondered horridly at what she'd done. But when Makk took his first breath, she knew she'd do anything to keep him with her. She'd do anything to protect him.

Even if it meant destroying the entire Kingdom of Coeur to make sure no harm ever came to him again.

A fierceness bubbled up inside her. No one, no thing would stand in her way. She'd make sure of it.

So as the roiling inky liquid coursed through her veins, she made a vow to the power she'd been gifted, to claim it all, seize it all, and use it all to create the only environment in which she could protect her Makk—one where she was queen.

Kierra blinked the memories away, returning her focus to the Sea of Oorbara. She planted her one human foot more firmly in the sand, and without looking at the griffin, reached her frog hand back toward him and said, "Bring me my saddle bag." The griffin approached, stopped beside her, and turned so she could reach the satchel attached to the saddle he wore.

Kierra unfastened the leather straps and removed a crystal bowl carved from black onyx, its smooth surface veined with streaks of smoky gray. She stepped into the sea, allowing the gentle lapping waters to encircle her ankles. Stooping, she dipped the bowl in the salty waves and scooped a measure of ocean into the vessel.

"Stand back," she commanded the griffin.

Tucking his wings against his body, the chimera shuffled backward with its powerful legs.

With her frog hand, Kierra held the bowl; with her human hand, she reached up to touch the pendant at her neck—the razor-tipped talon of a hawk. With a wince, she dragged the tip of her finger over its honed point, producing a single drop of blood.

Holding her finger in front of her, she pressed her thumb directly below the puncture, allowing the liquid to bubble up, black and glimmering.

It had been years since her blood had been red.

Turning her finger over the bowl, Kierra dripped one drop of Bitter into the ocean water.

A boom pulsed through the air, through the sea, rippling like the water in the bowl she held.

Silence enveloped the beach.

Then a subtle rumble of distant thunder.

Tentacles of gray clouds approached from the left and right, snatching the light from the sky, grasping the sun and overturning it into a sea of dark storm clouds.

Cupping the bowl in both hands, Kierra rolled her shoulders back, then down, and lifted her face to the darkened sky.

"Come, oh bitter creatures of mine," she chanted. "Heed the call of your queen divine." The water in the bowl rippled with the syllables of each word. The sea around her writhed in rhythm. "The time has come to protect your home," she declared. "And ensure your queen upon the throne."

Through the power of her Bitter bonds formed with each creature she'd made, she called to them, summoned them with her dark magic.

"Like calls unto like," she declared. "Sea unto sea, Bitter unto Bitter. Come forth. Your master has spoken."

Violent waves crashed against the shore, each one larger than the first.

The dark clouds flashed with lightning. Wind roared with rage. Then she saw them.

Amid the chaos of the churning sea, she witnessed the distinct flutter of winglike appendages.

The school of stingray chimeras raced toward the shore, then halted mere feet from the queen. The shallow waters writhed with their flapping. The horrific creatures peered up at her with their grotesque faces, many mixed with other ferocious sea creatures: the jaws of sharks and eels, the poison-tipped spines of sea urchins, the stinging tentacles of jellyfish, and the saber bills of swordfish.

With two hands, Kierra lifted the bowl of Bitter-tainted ocean water over her head.

"A threat has come to our kingdom," she declared over the roaring waves. "A threat to your queen," she added, knowing the loyalty ran as deep as the dark Bitter in their veins. "A traitorous group of individuals, Reds who bear the Eylan—the Eylan that rightfully belongs to your queen."

As if in agreement, the stingray chimeras slapped the waves in wet applause.

"You know the honors promised to those who seize the remnants of this power."

She heard the griffin on the beach behind her make a low chortling sound.

"Glory!" she shouted. "Honor and praise! A laurel crown and the right to sit upon the throne of our expanded kingdom as my ambassador."

Another boom pulsed through the realm, rippling both the water in the bowl and the sea.

Lightning split the sky.

Thunder crackled.

"Now go forth, my creation! Subdue this kingdom, bringing it under the authority of your queen. Reclaim my power, and eliminate all threats—at any cost."

Once again, the watery applause of the creatures splashed around her, and just as quickly as they'd heeded the summons, the chimeras withdrew to the depths of the sea, thrashing the waves with their retreat.

The entire Sea of Oorbara roiled like the Bitter in her veins, the sky as dark as that inky substance. With one final whisper of a curse, she dumped the contents of the bowl back into the ocean.

The sea exploded.

Water surged upward like a geyser, changing the direction of the currents. Waves raced away from shore instead of toward it, creating a violent suctioning sound as the tide receded. The storm clouds above followed, seeking those who threatened their queen.

Kierra wiped her hands on the pants of her riding leathers, turned, then hobbled back toward the griffin. She forced herself to walk as evenly as she could, not allowing him to see the strength the conjuring had drained from her. With tight lips, she eased the bowl back into the saddle bag and removed the tiny vial Fia had packed for her. She uncorked it and swigged its contents.

The griffin watched her with a piercing stare. "That was . . . spectacular, my crown," he finally said. "But why here? Why did we need to come all the way to Oorbara when the girl and the Reds were last seen in Rasalas?"

Kierra wiped her mouth with the back of her frog hand, bristling as she always did at the cold, amphibious skin.

More and more that coldness seeped much deeper.

Into her bones.

Into her heart.

And though she'd just unleashed the terrors of the sea upon her enemies, she couldn't deny the sinking, swirling energy that spiraled inside her— fear that somehow her power would be stripped from her, taking with it her kingdom.

Her crown.

Her Makk.

Kierra narrowed her cat eyes at the griffin and pushed loose strands of hair away from her scaled face, wondering what all he'd truly seen in Rasalas.

"War is not just about knowing your enemy's current whereabouts and actions. You must anticipate their next move—and the next—to stay ahead of them." She considered the irony of the statement. "Come," she said as she mounted the saddle on his back. "We must return to the capital."

Poor blasted griffin, she thought as she strapped herself in. He had no idea he was about to meet the ammit.

CHAPTER SEVEN

THE NIGHT BEFORE THEIR DEPARTURE TO the next trove, Nora sat at a long wooden table in the town center, surrounded by her dogs, her new friends, and the residents of Arcadia. Delicious fragrances scented the air, wafting up from the banquet they'd prepared in her honor. A warm sensation spread through Nora's chest as she considered her gratitude for the Arcadians she'd met and the kindness and generosity they'd shown her over the past week. She'd fallen in love with the quaint, secret village and its humble residents, never guessing that in one of the most frigid and inhospitable landscapes of Coeur she'd encounter the most hospitable collection of beings.

For a full eight days Nora had dwelt with them, learning the ways of the Eylan. It didn't feel nearly long enough. But thankfully, after her experience of swimming in the frigid lake, learning and understanding came easier, quicker even. And thanks to her bond with Rowan and her ability to tap into his elemental power, Nora had learned to wield powerful air pulses on command, easily create air pockets as he'd once done for her, and command the winds to come and stay at will. She'd also mastered a few other skills, such as sending her voice on a breeze across broad distances, air deflection, and levitation—though she'd only successfully lifted small objects.

Aside from the grueling training schedule, Nora's visit to Arcadia had felt almost like a vacation. She'd eaten delicious meals prepared by Orella, enjoyed daily walks with Rowan and Fable—even Cassian and the other Reds had occasionally joined them. And she'd slept remarkably well, her body spent from hours of intense training with Numair, her mind at rest, knowing she had both Rowan and Fable tucked in beside her each night.

One evening over dinner, she'd asked Orella how it was possible for such a peaceful place to exist in such a hostile kingdom.

"Arcadia is an echo of what Coeur used to be," the rabbit had said. *"We are fortunate to have*

healers, such as Althea, who have staved off the worst effects of the Bitter, preserving our memory of what once was so we can manifest a future of what Coeur could still be."

Nora leaned forward and glanced down the long table to see only a few of the chimeras still seated. The others had gathered in circles of dance and music, a celebration of their forthcoming liberation and a send-off for Nora, who would leave in the morning.

Rowan climbed onto the bench beside her, then placed his front feet on the tabletop and barked in time to the music.

Nora smiled and draped her arm over him as she soaked in her final moments in Arcadia. Cobblestones covered the ground and radiated in a circular pattern. Quaint colorful cottages hedged in the communal space where tables had been set up, covered in a variety of food and drinks. Candles flickered on the tables while lanterns above shone their warm glow, strung up on ropes that zigzagged across the square.

The scene enchanted Nora with its magical

essence, reminding her of something out of a storybook.

Or a dream.

Nora still couldn't help but wonder if one day she'd wake up from this experience.

She hoped she never would.

Cassian sat on the bench across from Nora, notably silent as he pushed his food around his plate.

"What is it?" Nora asked.

"We used to have festivals like this in my home village. Celebrations and holidays."

Nora shifted.

Fable approached her from underneath the table and rested his chin on her knee. She could feel his drool seep into the fabric of her pants as he caught whiffs of food from her plate. She scratched the top of his head, then said to Cassian, "You must miss your family and home terribly."

"My family, yes," he said. "But my home is with the Reds now. And I do miss *them* greatly. I'm glad to have Eira and Taran with me."

Nora nodded, then after a long pause said, "I've been thinking. You shouldn't go with us to the next trove. You should go back to the Reds, to your home in Yarou."

He shook his head. Firelight from the lanterns above glimmered golden in his dark-brown curls. "I told Sadie I would look out for you."

"And you have. You helped me reach the first trove. You helped me find Fable. And it's just . . ." She pressed her lips together, then said, "It's dangerous for you. You don't have the Ey—"

"I know what I don't have," Cassian interrupted. "But I have my honor. I gave my word to Princess Sadie that I would see this journey through."

Nora chewed the inside of her lip and nodded.

Fable pressed the weight of his chin harder against Nora's knee. "Nora?"

Grateful for the interruption, she leaned back so she could see his face. "Yes?"

"I have something to show you!" His tail wagged, slapping the wooden table with loud thumps.

She returned her attention to Cassian, hoping her eyes communicated her apology. "I'll be back."

Cassian nodded but said nothing.

Rowan joined when Nora stood to follow Fable.

The sounds of lute and lyre faded as they passed the swarm of dancing chimeras, then strolled down the gravel path away from the village square.

Silence enveloped them as they walked farther from the festivities. The still night reminded Nora of when they'd first arrived in Arcadia. The memory of that night seized her, reawakening the fears she'd been actively overcoming the past several days during her training.

Fable had looked so hopeless then, so near death.

Now he trotted a few paces ahead of her, Rowan at his side. The long feathery fur on his tail swished back and forth. His toes kicked up gravel as he went. Despite the fears that tried to resurface, Nora could feel the joy emanating from Fable, the aliveness that trailed in his wake. Even more strongly, she could feel Rowan's peace and excitement travel down their bond. She wrapped her mind around the sensation, mentally pulling it toward her to make the cord visible. The bond between her and Rowan shone brightly through the night.

The band of liquid-light appeared much thicker than the first time she'd seen it, back on Mount Croia. Now she could visibly see the energetical current of Eylan surging through the connection. It flowed around Rowan's neck, his chest, no longer just a harness but a shield of light. The cord stretched from his body back toward her, firmly connected but with no tension. It swirled around her left wrist, encircled her forearm, and banded her bicep. Now the sleeve of liquid-light reached as far as half her chest. The warm buzz of energy sent ripples of power through her body.

I'm grateful, she whispered in her mind. And though they couldn't hear her as she spoke, she added, *I'm grateful to be here with you, Rowan, to be here with you, Fable. I'm grateful for this moment together.*

Fable glanced over his shoulder, as if Nora's silent words had reached him. He grinned with a broad golden retriever smile, then continued down the path.

When they reached the end of the trail, Fable led them past Orella's A-frame cottage and onto the pebbled beach. Nora followed her dogs across the cold stones until they reached the water's edge.

"What did you want to show me?" she asked Fable.

He wagged his tail and turned away from the water to face the direction they'd just come. "That!" He pointed his nose at the sky.

Nora followed his line of sight up the pebbled beach, tracing the line with her eyes all the way to the wooded area they'd passed through. She saw the trailhead to the left of Orella's cottage.

A heavy darkness blanketed the beach, making everything look as black and heavy as ink. But as her eyes adjusted, specks of stars became visible in the nighttime sky.

Nora felt her face soften with a smile. The moon, now a waning gibbous, peeked over the darkened points of the pines in the center of the island.

Rowan leaned against her left leg, Fable against her right. Her eyes narrowed on a ripple of illumination in the sky.

"What is that?" she asked, watching as misty bands of gold and red snaked through the sky in undulating waves.

Overcome by a sense of wonder, she knelt between her dogs and pulled them close.

"It's beautiful."

The bands of light thickened, swirled, then shuddered with a ripple as if a stone had been cast into the sky.

Not knowing why, Nora laughed.

The aerial display reminded her of the northern lights, though she'd only seen them in pictures and videos.

As she watched more closely, the streams of light seemed to ripple up from the center of the island, like curls of steam rising from a pot of boiling water.

"It's coming from the island," she said, pointing.

"No," Fable said, nudging her leg. "The island is pulling it closer."

And as he said it, she realized he was right. The currents of gold and red swirled down toward the island before soaring back up into the star-speckled sky.

"What is it?" she asked again.

Both of her dogs leaned heavily into her as Fable said, "A residue of the Eylan released by Rowan at the trove. What you're seeing is the Eylan Ether. No one has seen it for a very long time."

"Ether," Nora repeated. "Numair said it's an element."

"Yes," Fable said quietly. "A very old, ancient, and rare element."

Mesmerized, Nora slipped into a trance. For what felt like hours she sat on the cold beach between her dogs, staring at the hypnotic dance of illumination.

Her chest buzzed with energy. The tingling sensation traveled down both of her arms, through the core of her trunk, down her legs, and straight back up until the sensation alighted in the center of her forehead.

And for a moment, it felt as if her eyes were open for the very first time.

The red-golden colors of the Eylan deepened in vibrance. The light pulsed and swirled more rapidly, more rhythmically, until Nora swore she could hear long soulful notes through the air, as if the vibration of the Eylan formed a song. Its percussion vibrated through her body until she recognized it as the same song the chimeras played in the village square. And yet, it didn't come from the chimerical musicians.

The music came from the Eylan. The music *was* the Eylan. It synchronized with the thrum of energy in Nora's body, aligned itself with the pulse of her heartbeat, and matched the gentle lap of the waves against the shoreline, somehow synchronizing with each of the various percussions and sounds of nature.

Rowan let out a gleeful bark, and the air around him rippled with light. Nora shuddered, feeling the sensation shoot through their bond. Fable released his own bark, then a howl. The atmosphere directly above their heads exploded with light, as if her dogs had called the currents of Eylan toward them.

And then, they were running.

All three of them.

Up and down the beach, Nora laughing, her dogs barking, as streams of Eylan curled around their bodies, grasping for them, parting as they raced through. Joyful tears streaked Nora's cheeks. She'd never felt so happy, so alive, so free. She stopped, thrust her arms out to the sides, and twirled as a whirlpool of Eylan swirled around her, starting at her feet and spiraling up, up, up. The top of the glowing funnel burst directly above her head in a full column of light. It exploded upward, struck the sky as if it were lightning, then surged back down.

Nora turned her face to the sky just in time to see the column of light collide into her. It pierced her forehead, alighted in her head, then surged down her spinal column. She gasped, breathing it in. Golden light consumed her vision, flecked with red glimmers.

It surrounded her.

It filled her.

It *was* her.

And she was it.

She reached out a cautious hand and touched the thick substance. Liquid-light coated her fingers. The Eylan rippled as she swiped her hand through it. She laughed again.

Beside her, Fable and Rowan flopped onto the ground and rolled onto their backs, kicking their legs into the air while wiggling back and forth. Currents of Eylan swirled around their feet, responding to their dance.

Nora recognized the playful behavior she'd seen her dogs perform a hundred times, then remembered seeing Princess Sadie's pack engage in the same gleeful activity when Nora first arrived in Coeur. Even the residents of Arcadia participated, Nora realized, thinking of the vibrant dancing that took place in the center of the village. They were all dancing in the Eylan, though not the fullness of it. Only a small residue of what had been unleashed at the first trove.

Overwhelmed, Nora allowed herself to envision what the Kingdom of Coeur might look like once they'd unleashed the Eylan at all three troves and returned the aurei to the Temple of Eylan.

She dropped to the ground and hugged her knees to her chest, watching the mystical display.

Her throat tightened. The beauty of the vision filled her mind, while the vision of her dogs—both of them—dancing in the Eylan captured her eyes.

Her skin sizzled with energy. Her insides roiled with the vibration of an emotion so pure she knew it had to be the truest magic of life.

"The Eylan," she breathed.

She soaked in the moment, soaked in the liquid-light, allowing it to seep into her pores.

Eventually, Rowan and Fable fell still, as if they, too, now wholly absorbed the atmosphere around them.

After some time, the light dimmed. The currents of red and gold faded. And the starry night sky was the only thing visible once again.

Nora turned to face the water. Golden stars reflected off its inky surface, winking as if to remind her of the magic she'd just witnessed.

Footsteps crunched in the stones behind her.

"There you are."

Cassian's voice.

Nora turned to see him approach with Eira, Taran, and Orella.

The Reds wore gleeful expressions and exchanged knowing glances with Rowan and Fable.

"We have another surprise for you!" Fable said.

Orella smiled and motioned for Nora to follow her down the beach.

The animals led the way, and Nora fell in step with Cassian.

"I'm sorry for what I said earlier," Nora said.

Cassian shrugged. "Don't worry about it."

"It's just . . . I don't want you to get hurt. I have Rowan, Eira, and Taran to help me at the next trove. And Fable," she added.

"Yes, but you said it yourself: I'm good with a bow and arrow."

"Yes, but I know how to wield now," Nora said. "I don't want you to feel like you have to come just because you made a promise to Princess Sadie."

Cassian stopped and turned to face her. The Reds and Orella continued down the beach, not noticing.

"Did it ever occur to you that maybe I'm not just here for you?" Cassian asked.

Nora pressed her lips together. "No."

"So you never considered that maybe this quest fulfills something deep inside me as well? That maybe this is my journey too?"

"I'm sorry, I—"

"Don't be sorry, Nora. Just open your eyes. The Eylan is about bonds and relationships, and there's more than one around you."

His words cut her.

"Besides," he said, lightening his tone, as if he'd realized how heavily his words had landed. "What if at the end of this entire journey you discover that what you really need to save Coeur is an extra set of thumbs?" He wiggled his fingers in her face.

Nora forced a smile, but his words lingered. She followed him in silence as they caught up to Orella and the dogs.

The beach curved inward, leading them into a cove. Nora stopped when she saw what was waiting for them.

The residents of Arcadia had gathered at the water's edge, each holding a glowing paper lantern in their hands. The flickers of light reflected off the water and illuminated a small sailboat.

"What is this?" Nora asked.

"It was Cassian's idea," Orella said as she scampered to Nora's side. "He said they used to have send-offs like this in his childhood home in the Kingdom of Smyredia."

Nora turned to him. "You did this? But I thought we were leaving in the morning."

Cassian's gaze remained fixed on the sailboat as he spoke. "Where I'm from, the fishermen and sea merchants were our heroes. They're the ones who sustained our coastal kingdom and made it thrive. The kingdom depended on them." His throat bobbed as he swallowed. "A hero always deserves a proper send-off." His eyes slid to hers. "We're leaving tonight."

A mix of emotions fell heavily on Nora as she considered his words, their meaning, and the fact that she was mere minutes away from leaving the haven of Arcadia. Suddenly, she didn't feel ready.

A subtle sensation swirled in her chest, like a vortex, and she recognized the low emotions threatening to pull her down. She sucked in a deep breath, forced a smile onto her face, then said,

"Thank you, Cassian. I'm grateful to have you with me on this journey. And thank you for this send-off. It's magical."

A smirk curled on Cassian's lips. "Oh, this isn't for you," he said. "I did it for Rowan, Eidolon of Coeur." He winked. "Everyone loves him here."

Nora burst with laughter, the awkwardness between them banished.

"Well, he's definitely my hero," she said. "But he doesn't have thumbs." She winked back at Cassian, then pushed past him to board the small sailing vessel. Rowan, Fable, Eira, and Taran were already on board.

When she reached the base of the ramp that led from the beach to the boat's top deck, Numair stopped her, Althea at her side.

"It has been my great honor to get to know you, Nora. You and your dogs."

Nora sucked in a shaky breath, then slowly let it out. "I don't feel ready."

"Of course you don't," Numair said. "That's because you're not ready."

Nora wrinkled her brow.

"No one is ever fully prepared for the journey that awaits them. But you are as ready as you need to be in this moment. Your journey will prepare you the rest of the way. Of that I am certain."

The panther-woman held out her open arms, then folded Nora into a hug. Warmth washed over Nora as she realized this human-hybrid was her friend. And so were Cassian, Eira, Taran, and Orella. Even Arcturus and many of the other chimeras she'd met in Arcadia.

Cassian was right. Though they weren't the same as her bond with Rowan, she'd made several new connections and relationships in Coeur.

Numair pulled away and scanned Nora's face with her yellow cat eyes. "What is it?"

Emotion threatened to choke Nora's words, but she said, "I feel at home."

Numair placed her hands on Nora's shoulders. "Of course you do," she said. "That's because it is your home."

Nora nodded, then glanced over her shoulder at Rowan and Fable, who peered over the rail of the small sailing vessel, watching her with adorable expressions.

"Yes," she said. "My home is with them."

Numair squeezed Nora's hands, then released her. "We're counting on you, Nora. And we believe in you."

Orella joined them. Arcturus, Edric, and Quince approached behind her. Nora took a moment to say goodbye to each one, along with a few of the other chimeras who paused to bid her farewell and good luck. Afterward, Orella motioned for Nora to crouch down to her level.

The cottontail rabbit wore a woolen dress with floral print and two yellow ribbons tied in bows around the base of each of her long ears. Nora almost forgot she was an oracle and not an adorable stuffed animal, until the rabbit spoke.

"You've learned much with Numair over the past eight days," she began. "Trust your training, and trust Rowan."

"I will," Nora replied.

"Good. Now, if I may send you off with a few parting nibbles of wisdom . . ."

Nora smiled, then nodded for her to continue.

"We oracles have very little Eylan, but what we lack in power, we make up for with our insight into the ways of the Eylan. Which is why we've always stuck close to the Reds. We need each other. We all do. What we find lacking in ourselves, we can often find in another. Which is all part of the great fractal design, which you'll soon see depicted in the mandala at the Temple of Eylan."

Nora drew in a deep inhale, amazed at the trust and confidence this small creature placed in her.

"You'll get there, Nora," Orella said. "You *will* save this kingdom."

"Do you know that because you're an oracle? Because you can see the future?"

Orella uttered a soft chuckle. Her lips parted, revealing buckteeth. "No, no." She reached out with her soft paw and took Nora's hand. "Being an oracle is not so much about seeing into the past or future; it's about seeing into the heart of another." She placed her paw on Nora's chest. "I see you, Nora. And now it's time for you to see yourself."

The rabbit's words stirred something inside Nora, though she couldn't place it.

"And," Orella added, "you must learn that love never dies; it only changes form." She paused. "You are learning the ways of love—the ways of the Eylan. But never forget that the Eylan is much more than a magical force to wield. It *is* love—the essence of life. And you, Nora, must learn how to live and love again."

The rabbit's words tugged at Nora's mind, her heart, but their understanding still eluded her.

With a final pat on Nora's chest, Orella removed her paw and said, "Don't worry. All of these things shall be revealed to you." She winked. "I *know* they will. After all, I'm an oracle. I know things." She hopped a step back. "Now off you go."

"Thank you," Nora said, then thought to ask, "How will I know where I'm going?"

Cassian approached. "Orella has already given me the map." He waved a piece of rolled up, wax-coated parchment through the air.

"And once we find the trove, how do we know where to go next? Will there be a . . .?" She tried to remember what Arcturus had called himself. "A trove guardian there to take us to the last oracle?"

Hearing the discussion, Arcturus joined them. The tiny rabbit leaned back against the beastly sky lion's paw.

"You catch on quickly," Orella said. "Yes, we are quite grateful for our committed servants." She patted Arcturus's taloned foot. "The trove guardians have each made a huge sacrifice, all for the sake of a great cause: to see the Kingdom of Coeur made whole." She reached forward one last time and touched Nora's leg. "We believe in you."

With that final word from the oracle, Nora mounted the ramp to the boat, Cassian behind her. He untied the lines that moored the small vessel to shore.

The residents of Arcadia stepped to the water's edge with their lanterns and placed them onto the inky-black surface. The waters lit with the warm reflection.

Nora watched as Cassian went to work preparing the sails.

The lanterns surrounded them, some even floating ahead on the current as if leading the way.

The dots of light lit up the night, and a soulful song filled a gentle breeze.

Nora glanced at Rowan, who stood beside her, commanding gentle winds to carry them out of the cove into the center of the lake.

After raising the sails, Cassian came to stand beside her. "Looks like you don't just need someone with thumbs. You need someone who knows how to sail."

A soft smile pulled at her lips. "Thank you," Nora said into the wind.

"You're welcome."

The Arcadians' song filled the night and followed the sailboat on Rowan's breeze, as did the dozens of golden glowing lanterns.

"Orella said there is a narrow passage through the mountains where the lake meets the sea," Cassian said. "I'll sail us there through the night. You should get some rest. We have a long journey ahead of us."

Nora waved a final farewell from the stern of the boat, then made her way to the bow where Fable stood, staring out over the open waters. She paused beside him and patted his head.

"Are you wishing you had your Eylan right now?"

He looked up at her with a confused expression. "How could I wish for that when I have you?"

His words warmed her heart, reminding her that he'd once said something similar. "You do have me," she said and sat beside him. "And I have you." She sucked in a deep breath of the night air. "I'm so grateful I have you."

As she wrapped her arms around him, she felt a fluttering in her chest. Not the same flutter she felt with Rowan's bond, but a distinct swell of love.

"Look," he said.

She followed the turn of his face with her stare, peering up at the night sky where brilliant stars glimmered on a blanket of black velvet. Swirls of the Eylan Ether smeared the darkness.

"It's even more beautiful out here."

Fable leaned harder into her, the weight and presence of his body somehow becoming even more real and tangible.

"I love you, Fable," she said, the words choking. "Do you know how desperately I wished to tell you that after you passed?"

"I do," he said. "Because I heard it every time you said it."

"You did?"

"Not with my ears," he said. "With my heart."

She kissed the top of his head, her tears spilling over into his fur.

Rowan came to join them, and together, the three of them stared out at the Eylan-swirled sky, where stars and lanterns mirrored one another, guiding them forward through the night.

She wrapped her other arm around Rowan. "I'm so grateful for you both," she said. "I'm so grateful to hold *both* of you again."

And as she said it, a powerful gust of wind filled their sails and propelled them across the water.

CHAPTER EIGHT

QUEEN KIERRA SAT AT HER DRESSING table in her bedroom. Surrounded once again by the silk fabrics and finery of the castle, wiped clean of the grime from traveling to the Sea of Oorbara and back, she felt almost human again.

In the mirror, she saw a smirk tug at her reflection's lips.

"Almost human," she whispered.

She stared at her reflection a moment longer. It had been eight days since she'd seen it. The normally vibrant blue fish scales on her cheek and forehead looked paler than normal, like the fish chimeras held on ice at the market. Even her cat eyes shone with a dull green. She touched a hand to her forehead, feeling the nub of a second antler sprouting. No wonder she'd had so many headaches lately.

Makk twitched at her feet where he slept. She reached down and stroked his scaled back. "I missed you," she said in a soft voice, then slid her bare human foot along the soft feathers of one of his wings.

He sighed contentedly.

A gentle knock rapped on the bedroom door.

Kierra watched the entryway through the reflection in the mirror. "Come in."

Makk stirred and lifted his head.

The door creaked open.

"Fia," Kierra said, seeing the hybrid-woman.

"Welcome home, my crown," she said. "I hope you enjoyed your bath." She clutched her hands together at her waist and spoke too fast. "I've sent your riding leathers to the washroom and ordered your dinner to be delivered to your rooms. I know how exhausted you must be after your travels. Oh, which reminds me. I have your nightly dose."

"Bring it to me."

Fia crossed the room with short choppy steps, then pressed a cold vial into Kierra's amphibious palm. Makk sat up to watch as she uncorked it and drank.

She sighed in relief.

"Better, my crown?" Fia asked.

"Much." Kierra leaned back in the velvet-lined chair.

Fia picked up the hairbrush off the dressing table and began running it through the damp tendrils of Kierra's freshly washed hair. The queen sat silently, stroking Makk's head, wishing she never had to leave him.

After conjuring the curse at the Sea of Oorbara, she'd pushed Thorne to make haste in their return, eager to be reunited with her beloved dog. During the flight back, she'd felt the distinct energetic pulses that signaled the use of the Eylan.

The girl and the Reds were still out there, still wielding.

But not for long.

Kierra sighed, feeling her fear ebb at knowing she'd secured the second trove. Tomorrow she'd make preparations to visit the third and bolster its defenses.

Though she didn't need to.

The territory of Eblor would devour any intruder—just as its residents devoured their own kind.

She smiled at her reflection.

Her creations would soon eliminate the threat of the girl.

Just as certainly as the girl would lead Kierra to the remainder of the Reds.

Fia interrupted her thoughts. "I spoke to Caldon right before coming to your room," she said.

"And?" Kierra asked, realizing she hadn't spoken to the adviser yet. She and Thorne had returned late in the day. And she'd been eager to see Makk.

"The drift of griffins you sent to Yarou has returned."

Hard lines formed on Kierra's brow. "Eight days later?"

Fia's frightened face looked more like a chicken's than ever. "Yes, well, I mean they returned two days ago, but you weren't here so . . ." She cleared her throat. "They think they've found something."

"They think they've found something," Kierra repeated in a mutter, beyond enraged that Caldon hadn't taken the initiative to give the griffins their next orders. Then again, she'd chosen the hybrid adviser not for his ambition but for his submission.

"Well, clear my schedule for the morning, then, and tell Caldon not to be late."

"Yes, my crown."

They sat in silence as Fia finished brushing Kierra's hair, then began styling it into a loose braid for bed.

Kierra broke the silence. "Fia?"

"Yes, my crown?"

"Where is the griffin Thorne?"

Fia caught her gaze in the mirror. "At the stables. As you asked. Being groomed and fed."

"Good," Kierra said, not dropping Fia's stare as the hybrid-woman tied a ribbon on the end of her braid.

"And how is the ammit?"

Fia's fingers stopped. Her chest rose almost imperceptibly. "Hungry, my crown."

Kierra's lips curled into a smile. "How hungry?"

"Quite."

Makk shifted.

"Good. Let's give him a few more days to work up a *full* appetite. In the meantime, please ensure Thorne is given a royal welcome home."

Fia fingered the end of the braid. "So . . . place him in one of the private chambers in the western wing."

"You know the routine," Kierra said. "Let him think he's being rewarded for his honorable deeds. And offer him as much food as he'd like to plump his belly. After all"—Kierra shrugged—"you said the ammit is hungry."

The blazing late afternoon sun of the southern skies of Coeur beat down on Nora's bare shoulders. She squinted at it, eager for the moment it dipped beneath the horizon and gave her a reprieve. She'd ripped the sleeves from one of her thinner linen tunics as she'd seen Cassian do, saving the scraps of fabric to tie around her head as a cool covering. But it didn't help much. She'd always tanned easily, but after almost two full days on a sailboat on the open water with little reprieve from the sun, her skin had taken on a distinct pink color.

"Look!" Rowan said excitedly. "You're a Red like us!"

Cassian chuckled as he adjusted the sails. His olive skin had darkened without so much as a hint of sunburn.

"Looks like the Eylan doesn't do much for heat," Nora joked, "only cold."

Cassian scrutinized her bare arms with his dark-brown eyes. "Oh no," he said. "You'd be blistering by now if not for the Eylan."

"But what about you?" she asked. "You're not burning."

"You're forgetting I grew up in Smyredia, one of the southern kingdoms on the continent, then moved to Oorbara. I'm used to the sun."

It wasn't the first time Nora had considered the fact that they were on a completely different continent than North America—and on a completely different planet in an entirely different realm. But the thought still boggled her mind. And though she'd glanced at the map multiple times since the moment they'd departed Arcadia, she asked Cassian to see it again.

"So where are we now, and how much farther do we have to go?"

Cassian stepped away from the main sail and pulled out the map Orella had given them, unrolling the wax-coated parchment.

He pointed to the northernmost part of the continent, in the general area of Arcadia, then traced his finger along the right side of the page. "Probably somewhere around here," he said, pointing to a spot on the coast of Yarou.

"Yarou?" Nora said. "We're close to Princess Sadie and the Reds?"

Cassian chuckled. "Close? I wouldn't say that. We're a long way out at sea. But yes, if my navigation is correct, we're not far from one of the two rivers that connect back inland and feed into Yarou Lake. Though we could be much farther south. It's hard to be precise since we've been using the Eylan."

Nora stared at the map. "So Coeur makes up the upper half of the continent?"

Cassian nodded. "And will make up the *entire* continent if Queen Kierra has her way. Only the southern kingdoms of Valecrest and Smyredia managed to escape her reign. And they've paid for it dearly."

"I bet you wish you were still in Smyredia," Nora said.

"Maybe. But if that were the case, I'd never have met the Reds. Or you."

Nora couldn't be certain, but she thought his cheeks looked a little pink.

"Anyway," Cassian said, then cleared his throat, "here's Rasalas, where we found the first trove." He tapped the mountain range on the upper portion of the map. "And here's Oorbara, where we're headed, currently the southernmost territory of Coeur. We have to sail all the way around the eastern side of the continent to reach it."

"We still have so far to go," Nora groaned.

"Yes." Cassian rolled up the map and secured it in his satchel. "But it's not far for someone who has the Eylan on their side." He winked, then added, "And one of the best sailors in all of Coeur." He puffed out his chest, and Nora laughed.

Nora thought back to their first evening aboard the sailboat, almost a full forty-eight hours ago. Cassian had proven himself to be quite the captain, singlehandedly manning their small vessel through the narrow mountain passages of Arcadia until they'd reached the open ocean. By the afternoon of their first full day at sea, he'd said, "All right, I'm ready for you."

Nora tapped a hand to her chest. "Me?"

"Yes, you. Do you see any other human wielders around here?"

She fingered the ends of her braid and chewed her lip.

"Time to use the Eylan, Nora," Cassian said.

Rowan nudged her hand with his nose. "I'm ready too!" he said.

Fable licked her other hand encouragingly. "You can do it."

"We'll all pitch in," Eira had added. "I'll carve the waves so the currents favor us. Taran will keep the storms at bay, and Nora and Rowan, you can propel us with the winds."

"And I'll steer," Cassian had said. "We should reach the second trove in five or six days, maybe sooner. Now if you don't mind . . ." He gestured for Nora to take her place at the stern.

At the back of the small sailing vessel, Nora stared at their wake as it faded into the distance. Rowan and Fable stood beside her, one on either side. She closed her eyes and focused on the hum of energy she felt coursing between her and Rowan, narrowing her attention on it, feeling its strength pulse from her chest and down her left arm where Rowan stood, wishing she'd felt a similar sensation on her right as well.

When she opened her eyes, a burning golden thread stretched from her to Rowan, but between her and Fable, there was nothing. He'd looked up at her with expectant, golden eyes. And though so much dread and fear still swirled inside her, she couldn't deny the overwhelming warmth that swelled in her chest as she gazed upon her beloved dog.

Alive.

Whole.

Present.

She'd blinked back tears, then turned to face Rowan. He, too, stared at her with a look of pure adoration and loyalty. And for a brief moment, she forgot their lives were at stake, forgot that she'd somehow been transported into a mystical realm and that her parents had no clue where she was or what was happening to her.

Instead, she felt like the luckiest girl in the world to be on an adventure with her two best friends.

The emotion had swelled and intensified, flooding her body with a buzzing warmth. She focused on the feeling and concentrated on expanding it, flooding herself with memories of her two dogs and all the adventures they'd shared.

And would share.

The buzzing had turned into a hum, then a raging current of energy. Nora's entire body had tingled with pins and needles, like the sensation of blood flowing back into a leg that had fallen asleep. The glowing bond of Eylan between her and Rowan had burned brightly, then thickened.

Turning her attention skyward, Nora shouted, "Wind, come!"

And it did.

A forceful gust shoved against her, whipping her braid off her shoulder. She'd turned in time to see the sails catch and fill with air. Cassian glanced up at her from where he crouched near the boom, grinning.

The sailboat sliced through the water.

Eira barked joyfully from the bow, and the surface of the sea split, creating two curls of water that peeled away, leaving nothing but a glasslike path in front of them.

Taran had turned his nose skyward and searched for approaching storms, while Cassian continued to direct their vessel.

Nora had remained at the stern with Rowan and Fable, guiding the currents of air, calling them to come stronger and faster.

They'd covered as much distance as possible that day, slowing only at dusk to eat the provisions Orella had packed for them: strange, dried fruits and hard cheeses, plus clay containers of various stews and porridges. They'd rationed everything carefully, except for Taran, who'd managed to convince Cassian for seconds with his pleading eyes.

"No meat," Nora had commented absently as she tore off a hunk of sourdough from a loaf Orella had packed, then realized what she'd said.

Cassian shook his head. "It's not advised to eat chimeric meats. At least, not for those of us who are still loyal to the Eylan. The Bitter is in the blood."

Nora had scrunched up her nose.

"Besides, we don't need it. Orella packed plenty of healthy foods." He pulled out a pouch of dried fruits. "This is the keddu fruit. It grows underground like a beet or a carrot and is quite hardy, which is why the Rebels can grow them in such cold conditions." He'd popped one into his mouth, then handed one to Nora.

"Where does the cheese come from?" she asked while chewing.

Cassian shifted. "It's probably best if you don't know."

When she stopped chewing, he chuckled.

"The Bitter doesn't pass through an animal's milk," he said. "That's all you need to know."

Nora resumed her chewing but avoided the cheese for the rest of the meal.

That second night, Cassian had shown Nora the bare basics of how to sail the boat, informing her that he'd need the most sleep out of the six of them. While the Eylan would extend the Reds' and Nora's physical energy, Cassian was still bound by his human limits, and Nora would need to take the helm from time to time.

He'd stayed awake as long as possible that night, watching Nora at the wheel, coaching her, and answering questions. But eventually he'd fallen silent, and when Nora had turned to look at him, he was slumped against the side of the boat, still seated upright but fast asleep.

Nora smiled now, recalling the memory from the night before, savoring the joy of the journey thus far, then handed the map back to Cassian. "So, what, another three days till we reach the trove?" she asked.

Cassian eyed the map, then rolled it up. He returned her smile. "With you and Rowan, I think we can do it in two."

CHAPTER NINE

E VEN AFTER FOUR DAYS AT SEA, NORA hadn't lost the wonder of watching the sun ascend the horizon. She marveled at the way the flaming-orange orb popped up from the depths each morning. The sight renewed her energy. Though, she had to admit, that energy—her Eylan— felt increasingly drained the farther they traveled and the closer they got to the next trove. Nora swore she could feel that hoard of power calling to her with a humming resonance.

She watched Cassian from where she stood at the wheel, steering, while he adjusted the sails. The sun, now slightly higher in the sky, warmed his tanned skin. The four Reds glowed in the morning light, their coppery fur reflecting the sun's radiance.

Nerves fluttered in Nora's belly. She swallowed, feeling an anticipatory swell of energy wash over her skin. "We're close," she said so quietly only she could hear.

Cassian joined her. "Weather looks good today. We've been making great time."

"Maybe too great."

He gave her a questioning look. "What do you mean?"

She sighed. "I'm just not ready to face the next trove yet."

He took the wheel from her. "Well, you'd better get ready. If we keep this pace, we should come upon the trove later today or tomorrow."

"Today?"

"Or tomorrow," he repeated. "Don't worry, Nora. Remember what it does to your energy."

"Easier said than done." She closed her eyes and drew in a deep, steadying breath of the salty air.

Taran released a bellowing bark from the bow of their small sailing vessel.

Nora's eyes snapped open.

He barked again, and this time she witnessed the streams of Eylan ripple from his mouth like sound waves. The golden threads bounced over the surface of the water, reached for the horizon, then pierced the distant sky.

Nora approached, leaving Cassian at the wheel. Rowan glanced at her over his shoulder from where he stood at the stern, holding a steady current of wind to fill the sails. Fable left his side to follow Nora.

"What's up?" Nora asked Taran.

"A storm," he said. "It's still a ways off, but I can sense it."

"How can you tell?"

"I can feel it in my belly."

"Are you sure you're not just hungry?" Nora teased and scratched the top of his head.

Eira pushed Taran out of the way, stealing Nora's affection. The petite Red positioned herself directly in front of Nora and leaned back to get her ears scratched. She thumped her hind foot with delight, then froze. Eira jumped to all fours, placed her front paws on the bow of the sailboat, then barked.

Nora stilled, sensing something different in her tone.

"Taran is right," Eira said, the ear scratches forgotten.

Taran barked again, this time finishing it with a growl. "It's odd," he said, staring at the horizon. "When I first sensed the storm, it wasn't moving. I could feel it hovering over the sea, like it was waiting."

"Waiting?" Nora said. "Waiting for what?"

An icy gust of wind whipped over the bow of the boat.

Eira barked again, her voice higher pitched than normal.

Taran lifted his head and howled. Eylan fled his mouth in a long, thick current of golden light, shooting straight up until it touched the wispy morning clouds above them. The Eylan struck like lightning, then spiderwebbed across the sky.

Another rush of frigid air shoved at them.

"I think it's waiting for us," Taran said.

The sailboat bounced on the waves.

"Eira?" Nora said.

The female Red turned to face her. "Tell Cassian to prepare for rough water."

"C'mon, Fable." Nora patted her leg for him to follow.

"What's going on up there?" Cassian asked when they reached him.

"There's a storm ahead. Taran is warding it off, but Eira said to prepare for some rough water."

As she said it, the deck of the sailboat darkened.

"Whoa," Cassian said as they watched a thick line of charcoal-gray clouds advance across the sky.

The scent of rain filled the air, and the hairs on Nora's arms tingled with the energy in the atmosphere.

But it wasn't the Eylan.

Lightning flickered in the blanket of clouds— different from Taran's lightning.

A second later, thunder cracked. Nora jumped. Her hands flew to cover her ears. The storm sounded louder on the open sea, more threatening.

The sailboat lurched as the winds changed course.

Cassian grabbed the wheel. "Rowan, what's happening back there?" he called over his shoulder.

"I'm losing control," Rowan said. "This storm has a strange wind pattern. I'm struggling to rein it in."

"Keep trying!" Cassian said.

"No!" Nora shouted to Rowan, remembering her lesson with Numair. "Don't *try*, Rowan. Command it. You can do it."

"Good call," Cassian said with a wince.

"What do you want me to do?" she asked.

His full lips pressed into a tight line as his dark eyes watched Eira and Taran at the bow.

"This storm feels . . . different," he finally said.

"Taran said that too."

Another flash of lightning streaked through the sky, reflecting off the cloud-darkened waves. Its deafening crack rattled Nora's chest.

"I think we're up against much more than a storm," Cassian said.

The sailboat rose on the crest of a large wave, then slammed against the sea, nearly throwing Nora to the deck.

"Here. Take the wheel," he said.

"Where are you going?"

"I've got to get the storm jib up and reef the mainsail."

"What does that mean?" she asked.

"Just keep her steady," he said. "And do whatever you can to help Rowan control the winds. If we broach, we're in trouble."

Nora wanted to ask what broaching meant but decided it was best not to fill her mind with the specifics of their impending doom.

She gripped the wheel of the sailboat, her knuckles blanching under the strain.

Fable pressed himself against her right leg. "I'm here," he said. "I'm right here with you."

"Good. Stay close."

Rain began to fall in fat droplets, splattering the deck of the boat, mingling with the spray of the waves that slickened the wooden surface.

"Rowan!" Nora called over her shoulder above the roar of the wind. "How are you holding up?"

His voice sounded strained. "These winds are different." He grunted. "They're powered by an unnatural force. I don't know what, but—"

A violent gust caught the sail. The boat leaned.

Cassian and the Reds flattened themselves to the deck while Nora clung to the wheel.

Once the vessel righted, Cassian rushed to Nora's side, shoved her out of the way, and took the wheel.

"Help Rowan," he commanded.

"But I thought *you* needed my help."

"I do," he said. "I need you to control these winds or we're going to capsize."

Nora's eyes widened.

"Go!" He shoved her in the direction of the stern. "And stay away from anything metal. We're a target for lightning out here."

The sailboat rocked from side to side as she made her way back to join her dog. The horizon line tilted while waves beat the sides of their small vessel. The fat raindrops fell harder and faster, now sharp, slicing pelts. The temperature of the atmosphere dropped.

Nora gripped the rail at the stern to keep from being tossed to the deck.

Rowan stood facing their wake, all four feet rooted to the wet deck. Fable took up position beside him, planting himself as he saw his brother do. Rowan howled, calling in a forceful gale that shoved the boat in the right direction.

"Nice work!" Cassian yelled above the storm.

The once-beautiful blue sea now churned a murky gray, lined with whitecaps.

The opposing winds changed course again.

The waves battered them from multiple directions.

"A one-hundred-eighty-degree wind shift!" Cassian shouted. "It's like there's multiple storm systems battling each other."

"Or battling us," Nora said under her breath. Louder, she said, "Rowan, do what you can to create favorable winds for Cassian. I'm going to fight off these opposing air currents."

He uttered an agreeable yip, then lifted his face and howled. Bands of glowing liquid-light poured from his mouth, swept over the stern of the boat, then swirled and doubled back, creating a blustery but consistent source of air for Cassian to leverage.

More clouds rolled in, darkening the sky even further, leaving little light beyond the gnarled fingers of lightning that grasped at the sky and sea.

The thunder was deafening.

Drawing on the swelling energy of the bond, Nora thrust out her hands as she'd done in practice with Numair during her training in Arcadia. She didn't *try*, just flowed, releasing the dam that held back the river of Eylan inside her. Energy pulsed from her palms, creating a transparent, glowing barrier to shield their vessel from the opposing winds. Rowan called in an air current to push them away from the storm.

"Wind, come!" he commanded.

The sailboat sliced across the waves.

Fable cheered.

Cassian wiped a mix of sweat, rain, and sea spray from his forehead with the back of his arm. "Nicely done. Now, let's keep her on this course. With the power of an eidolon, we should be able to easily ride out the storm."

Nora's shoulders relaxed.

"Good job, Nora," Fable said.

"Thanks," she panted.

"Eira, can you do something about this rain?" Cassian asked. "Visibility is terrible."

"I *am* doing something about it," she said.

Nora could see the strain on her face. "I'm holding it back with all my strength."

Cassian and Nora exchanged glances.

"You sure we can outrun this storm?" Nora asked.

Cassian chewed his lip, then his eyes widened.

Nora followed the direction of his gaze.

They didn't need clear visibility to see what was coming.

A towering wave gained height as it crested toward them.

"Hold on!" Cassian shouted.

Nora felt the instant Eira released her hold on the rain to redirect her Eylan toward the wave.

The rain sliced against Nora's bare arms and stung her face.

Eira released six clipped barks that shot from her mouth like missiles of light. They formed a barricade in front of their boat.

The wave crashed against the barrier and dispersed, leaving shorter, choppy waves for their vessel to bounce over.

"Nice work, Eira!" Nora shouted.

Cassian continued to steer the sailboat while Rowan filled the sails and Nora, Eira, and Taran did their best to hold off the various elements of the storm.

Nora sucked in a breath through her nostrils, straining against the opposing winds that beat against the protective barricade of air she held around them. Her arms trembled under the exertion.

"Uh, Cassian . . ." Taran's voice carried from the bow of the boat. "We have a problem."

"Grab the wheel, Nora."

She obeyed, using one straining arm to hold the glowing barrier in place while grasping the wheel with her other hand.

She saw Cassian pause between Taran and Eira, his bare feet planted wide to steady himself on the rocking vessel. He gripped the rail and peered over, then backed away. He said something to the two Reds that Nora couldn't hear, then returned to take the wheel from her. His tanned face looked ashen.

"What is it?" Nora asked in a strained voice as she released the wheel and lifted her other arm to continue pushing back against the storm.

Cassian's chest rose and fell. "We have company."

"Company?"

Ice filled his voice. "Sea chimeras."

Nora blinked the spray from her eyes, recalling the hundred-legged sea monster that had broken free from the ice wall in the frozen gulch and attacked them.

"What do we do?" she asked.

Cassian glanced over his shoulder at Rowan, who continued to hold a favorable current of wind in place, shoving them as fast as he safely could out of the storm's reach—but directly toward the chimeras he couldn't see.

Cassian shook his head. "I—I don't know."

Nora's mind whirled as she searched her memory, her training, for any tactics that could help them out of this situation.

She couldn't think of anything. Fear began to tug at her resolve.

She sucked in a shaky breath and fixed her mind on one thought—Rowan, Eidolon of Coeur. He would know what to do.

She rushed to the stern of the vessel.

"Something's not right," Rowan said as soon as she reached his side.

"You're right," she said, her trust in him strengthening with the evidence of his wisdom. "We're under attack. Chimeras. We need to do something, but I don't know what."

He peered up at her through the pelting rain, squinting against the slicing droplets.

She knelt in front of him and reached for the aureus that hung from his neck. "You're an eidolon," Nora said, gripping the coin-sized medallion. "Your Eylan is stronger than all of ours."

"*Our* Eylan," he said. "My power is your power."

Nora nodded. "Yes, *our* power. But I still need you and your instincts to know what to do."

Nora could see the wheels turning behind his dark-brown eyes.

"Okay," he said. "I have an idea. But you'll need to trust me."

"I do trust you," she said.

"Okay, then, Fable . . ." Rowan spoke to his brother. "Do whatever you can to help Cassian. It's going to get rough."

"I've got it," Fable said, rushing to Cassian's side.

A pit formed in Nora's stomach. "But he doesn't have the Eylan," she started to protest.

"Exactly," Rowan said. "Which is why he needs to help Cassian. He's capable of much more than you think, Nora."

She bit her lip but nodded.

"Eira! Taran!" Rowan called the other two Reds to join them at the stern. "Follow my lead. You, too, Nora. Trust our bond. Feel into it. You'll know what to do."

As he said it, a horrifying creature breached the waves and launched itself onto the deck of their boat. Its winglike fins flapped against the deck with a wet slapping sound and thrashed its hammerhead-shark face back and forth, teeth bared.

Cassian barked orders to Fable, who grasped and tugged at the lines on the sails while the teenage boy reached for his bow, then sank an arrow into the monstrous fish.

It ceased its flopping, and Cassian shoved it overboard, careful to avoid its barbed tail. He glanced over the side of the boat, then peered up with wide eyes.

"The water is teeming with them!" Cassian shouted.

"Back to the wheel!" Rowan ordered.

Cassian obeyed and continued shouting commands to Fable.

Nora watched in awe as her dog helped sail the boat.

"Nora," Rowan said, "you need to release the barrier holding back the wind."

"What?"

"Trust me!" he said.

She nodded, then allowed the glowing Eylan barrier to fall.

The boat careened to one side.

A wave battered it from the other.

"We need to leverage the storm," Rowan shouted above the now-deafening wind. "We have to use it, not fight it!"

Eira and Taran nodded knowingly.

"To the bow!" Rowan commanded.

Nora followed the three Reds, wishing she had four feet to stabilize herself.

She reached the bow and gripped the rail.

Her mind fogged over as she looked down at the violent waves.

The water rippled with the writhing, slippery bodies of the monsters of the deep.

Rowan howled.

A strange sensation jolted their bond, a yielding sensation, as if Rowan no longer resisted the opposing forces. He welcomed them, called to them.

An eerie quiet followed in the wake of his howl, then the storm erupted, heeding his call.

Wind battered their small boat.

Eira and Taran pressed their bodies against Rowan's, one on either side. Temporary threads of liquid-light flickered among them, as if their powers were intertwining.

Another sea chimera flopped onto the deck, thrown by a particularly violent wave.

Nora turned to see it land near Fable's feet.

"Fable!" she shouted.

She felt her bond waver.

"Nora!" Rowan commanded. "Don't be afraid!"

But she couldn't tear her eyes from her powerless dog, who gripped a line in his teeth, tugging to control the sails.

The monster swung its long eel neck in Fable's direction.

An arrow pierced its head.

Nora exhaled, but the terror of seeing her dog nearly bitten lingered.

"I need your help, Nora!" Rowan shouted.

She turned to see a thin funnel of water spiraling no more than two hundred yards in front of their boat.

"What is that?"

"Our salvation!" Eira grunted. "Now help us!"

Nora focused on the bond, still feeling the strange yielding sensation, now mingled with two foreign energies she guessed to be Taran's and Eira's.

The boat rocked violently beneath her feet. She struggled to stay upright.

Even more, she struggled not to be afraid.

Fear grasped at her like the spindly fingers of lightning that clutched the sky.

Despite the unsteady surface beneath her feet, she closed her eyes, pouring all of her focus on the warmth that pulsed in her chest and down her left arm.

"I trust you, Rowan," she said under her breath. "I trust you."

She could feel the bond thickening, growing.

A familiar sensation rushed up her arm and ricocheted in her rib cage.

Rowan had tapped into the power of the aureus.

The Eylan they'd recovered from the first trove pulsed through her body with its signature resonance, threatening to burn if she resisted it.

So she didn't.

Nora aligned herself to the energy, riding it as if it were a wave.

A loud roar rumbled across the water, and when Nora opened her eyes, a giant water cyclone swirled in front of them. Wind spiraled on the surface of the ocean, throwing water in all directions. Nora turned her face upward, seeing the funnel reach to the ominous clouds.

Hail began to fall, missing the boat but pelting everything else around them.

The creatures in the water writhed.

Some of them roared, releasing blood-chilling screeches.

A fiery band of Eylan burst from Rowan's chest. Eira and Taran leaned harder against him, sandwiching his body between theirs.

Nora could feel his exhaustion.

She dropped to the deck and placed her hands on his back, feeling his taut muscles.

"I trust you, Rowan!" she shouted above the roar of the waterspout.

The funnel thickened. Liquid-light mingled with the cyclone and spiraled around it.

One of the chimeras swam too close and was instantly sucked up into the twister. The funnel threw it across the water and away from their boat.

A smile pulled at Nora's lips. "You did it!"

Inch by inch, the waterspout widened, and one by one, it picked up the chimeras and thrust them from their sailboat's path.

The waterspout carved a trail across the sea.

Nora heard Cassian cheer.

She turned to see him, one hand on the wheel, the other forming a fist in the air. Fable stood near the center mast, still gripping a line in his teeth.

Nora returned the victorious gesture, thrusting her fist into the air, then fell to the deck as a supernatural gust shoved the boat sideways.

Cassian's eyes widened.

The sailboat lurched.

And Fable fell overboard.

"No!" Fear rippled through Nora's scream. She ran to the side of the boat, prepared to jump over and into the water when Cassian's hand locked around her arm.

"Don't!" he said. "You'll die!"

"If I don't jump in, *he* will die!" she said. Then, remembering Fable's words to her back on the beach in Arcadia, she added, "And then I'll die too." She yanked her arm from his grasp. "I'll face my own death if it means there's a chance I can save him."

"Nora, don't!" Rowan shouted.

She felt their bond waver as he turned, distracted.

Her fear compounded every second Fable remained in the water.

The bond flickered.

"Nora! Don't jump. Trust me!" Rowan said. "I can save Fable! I need you up here."

Nora's voice cracked. "I'm sorry. I can't lose him again." And without another word, she dove headfirst off the edge of the boat.

The shock of her terror felt colder than the water as her body sliced through the surface.

She could no longer feel her bond with Rowan.

Only the horrific dread that drew her deeper and deeper into the depths of the sea.

The light of their bond winked out.

She kicked, swimming as fast as she could away from the sounds of muffled chaos above, searching for Fable.

The terror of losing him again deepened as she realized she'd abandoned her crew.

She'd abandoned Rowan.

A sickening feeling of regret mingled with her fear, washing her in shame.

She swam deeper.

Her emotions swirled as violently as the waterspout Rowan had conjured to save them.

A flash of lightning illuminated the murky waters.

And then she saw him.

A fanged monster swept past Fable's sinking body, narrowly missing him.

But the current pulled him deeper.

Deeper into a downward spiral.

Just like her energy.

Despite the overwhelming fear as she watched her dog sink beyond her grasp, her mind landed on one thought.

Rowan.

He could have saved Fable—would have—if she'd merely trusted.

But it was too late now.

Abandoning the hope of using any Eylan in her terror-stricken state, Nora swam as deep as she could, as fast as she could. Descending into darkness, until her hand grazed Fable's body. She locked her fingers around his collar.

But she couldn't pull him up.

Together they sank into darkness.

He was going to die.

They both were.

And still all she could think about was how she'd abandoned Rowan. How she'd failed to trust him, controlled by her own fear.

Grief overwhelmed her.

She was losing him.

Losing *both* of them.

The currents of the raging sea tugged on Nora's and Fable's bodies, reminding her of the sensation of sinking into the frigid waters of Arcadia.

The same powerless feeling returned.

Her mind drifted to Rowan once again. Even in the depths of the Arcadian lake he'd been with her. Even as she'd sank. Even as she'd failed. His presence had remained with her through their bond, though she hadn't been able to see or feel it.

And just when she'd thought she'd reached her own end, he'd saved her.

Saved her with a pocket of air.

Nora's mind cleared, granting her a small reprieve from her spiraling fear.

I'm sorry, Rowan, she said in her mind. *I love you. I'm still here, just as I know you're still here. And I still trust you can save us. All of us.*

A thin cord of light sparked to life, stretching from Nora's body up through the dark waters like a glowing fishing line.

She leaned into the sensation of the bond, allowing her energy to flow upward instead of spiraling downward.

The glowing line tightened.

As soon as it did, Nora clutched tighter to Fable's collar, then wielded with the other hand, arcing it through the dark waters to create a glowing air pocket big enough to envelop both her and Fable.

Once inside, she gasped.

And so did Fable.

She hugged him to her body.

"I'm here," he said. "I'm right here."

"You're here," she whispered against the top of his wet head as the pocket of air rapidly lifted them from the depths.

As soon as the bubble broke the surface and burst, Nora scanned her surroundings, searching for their boat.

But it was gone.

Replaced by the sailboat's wreckage.

CHAPTER TEN

"ROWAN!" NORA SCREAMED IN A SHRILL voice, no longer able to see her bond. "Rowan!" She sucked in short shallow breaths as she struggled to keep her head above the water. "Rowan! Where are you?"

Fable doggy-paddled beside her as they searched the sailboat's wreckage. "Don't be afraid," he said.

A wave crashed against them.

Nora longed to give in to the terror that flooded her body, but she knew Fable was right. She focused her mind on her bond with Rowan until she felt the warmth pulse in her chest.

This time, she sent his name on a breeze, seeking him out. "Rowan."

Several moments later, a breeze returned.

"Over here."

Gratitude swelled in her chest, and their bond reignited. The relief brought instant tears to her eyes.

174 | H. R. HUTZEL

"C'mon," she said to Fable, swimming to follow the bond.

They crossed the dark, choppy sea until they reached a large piece of the sailboat's hull, where Rowan, Eira, Taran, and Cassian had managed to pull themselves up out of the water.

Nora helped Fable onto the floating wood, then pulled herself up. She wrapped her arms around a soaking-wet Rowan.

"I'm sorry," she sobbed. "I'm so sorry! I couldn't lose Fable again."

Rowan rested his head on her shoulder.

Cassian grunted.

It was only then that Nora noticed the way he sprawled across the piece of wreckage, clutching his side.

"What happened?" She knelt beside him.

He lifted the hem of his soaked tunic.

A large gash slashed across the flesh of his abdomen, right below the scales that marked his ribs.

"The spine of one of the chimeras . . ." He gasped. "It got me."

Nora quickly scanned the rest of their group. "Is anyone else hurt?"

The Reds all shook their heads.

"What do we do?" she asked.

"There is nothing we can do," Eira said, "without a healer."

"Can't you heal him with your Eylan?" Nora protested. "Like Althea did for Fable? Or maybe Rowan can do something to help. He's an eidolon."

Taran shook his head. "An eidolon is not a healer." His voice fell as he looked at Eira. "And neither are we."

Nora chewed her lip, nodded, then said, "Then we have to get him to one."

"How?" Cassian asked. "We don't have a boat."

Nora's mind whirled as she tried to come up with a plan.

"We'll use the Eylan and this piece of wreckage. We'll find a way to sail back to Yarou—"

"No." Cassian gripped her arm, reminding her of the moment right before she'd plunged over the side of their boat to save Fable.

"Listen to me for once," he said.

His tone silenced her.

"We are far closer to the trove than Yarou. If you're going to use your Eylan and this scrap of wood for anything, you sail us there." He winced and sat up, then gently removed his shirt. A necrotic, black spiderweb of veins surrounded the wound.

"The injury won't kill me," he said as he tore his shirt and tied it around his abdomen. "But the Bitter is in my blood. Taran?"

The stout Red appeared at his side. He held a rolled piece of waxy parchment between his teeth.

Nora took it from him.

"We managed to save the map," Cassian said. "But little else."

"The storm is finally retreating," Taran said, though dark clouds still filled the sky.

"And the chimeras are gone," Eira added. "For now."

"We have no time to waste," Cassian said.

A heavy weight of shame washed over Nora again.

Cassian tightened the makeshift bandage. "Lean into your bond, Nora. Not away from it."

She nodded but said nothing, too overwhelmed that she'd put all of them in such danger.

"I had to save him," she mumbled.

Rowan finally spoke. "Of course you did. But there is a way to leap in fear and a way to leap in love . . ." His voice trailed off, and Nora could see the hurt that lingered in his eyes.

She nodded. "I'm sorry. Please teach me."

He licked her cheek. "Then trust me."

She hugged him.

"This is all quite touching," Cassian said with another grunt, "but we need to get to the trove." He leaned back on their flimsy raft. "And then you need to get me to a healer."

They floated for hours, their sense of time warped by the thick storm clouds that continued to blot out the daylight. Cassian lay on his back, groaning softly, watching the sky for any indication of the direction they traveled. Small gaps in the clouds provided periodic glimpses of the angle of the sun, then later, the stars. But thankfully, despite the pain and the Bitter that now flowed through his veins, Cassian still managed to keep them on course.

Rowan and Eira pushed their tiny scrap of salvation across the sea, together wielding the wind and waves, while Taran held the storms at bay. They moved much slower without a sail, but thanks to the waterspout the Reds had conjured before their boat had capsized, the chimeras didn't return.

Though every so often Nora swore she saw a creature slither through the water beneath the slab of wood on which they floated.

The journey provided too much time for her to ruminate on what had happened. And several hours into their travels, when Cassian had drifted into a restless sleep, Nora finally asked Rowan what had happened after she'd jumped over the side of the boat to save Fable.

He didn't answer right away, his nose pointed toward the sky where he controlled the wind currents to push their raft across the water.

Finally he said, "When you dove overboard, you stopped trusting me. You flooded our bond with fear, blocking the flow of power." His eyes slid to hers.

She swallowed.

Fable sat between them, listening.

Rowan shook his head. "Eira, Taran, and I lost control of the storm. The boat capsized."

Nora clenched her hands in her lap.

"Fortunately, because Eira and Taran aren't influenced by your emotions, they were able to redirect the twister before it sucked us in with the boat."

His words landed heavily on Nora.

"*My* emotions," she said. "*My* energy pulled me down—and the boat too."

"And all of us," Rowan said, though there was no hint of accusation in his voice. Just truth. "We are bound to the aureus now, bound to a tremendous channel of power. And the greater your potential for power, the greater your potential for destruction. The more you believe in our bond, Nora, the more your emotions affect it." He paused. "You've hardly seen what we're capable of together. Because you're so afraid."

Though her dog didn't accuse her, Nora accused herself.

She alone had caused their shipwreck and Cassian's injury.

"Fable was going to die," she said. She rested her hand on Fable's head. "I can't lose him again, Rowan. Just as I can't lose you."

Rowan lowered to his belly and shuffled across the wooden raft, inching closer to her. "Don't you see, Nora?" he said. "You're so afraid of death, you've never actually lived."

His words stirred her mind, but before she could speak, he added, "Love never dies, Nora. It only changes form."

"Did Orella tell you that?" she asked, realizing they were the same words the oracle had spoken to her on the eve of their send-off.

Rowan wrinkled his brow. "No. Why?"

"Because she said the same thing . . ." Nora's voice trailed off. "Well, if she didn't tell you, then how do you know that?"

"I just do," he said. "I know it because it's true."

He held her stare, his eyes filled with so much wisdom—*more* wisdom, now that he was an eidolon.

Nora breathed in the salty, stormy air.

"I didn't die, Nora. But you believed *I did."*

Fable's voice sounded so clearly in her mind she swore he was speaking beside her.

"I was reborn. And if you want to be with me, where I am, you must be reborn too."

His words stirred her soul, reminding her of the ancient Eylan chant. And though she felt certain the window had closed for the chimeras that had been harmed during the storm, Nora felt compelled to bless them.

She placed a hand over her chest. "Come, Eylan, on eternal wings," she whispered into the wind, using her bond with Rowan to send the words on a current of air. "Imbue these vessels, as Mother sings." She felt the pulse of her heart beneath her palm. "Embrace transition to endless grace." Her bond with Rowan fluttered to life, glowing vividly down her left arm toward him. "Return to source and divine embrace."

The familiar coursing energy burned in her chest, the sensation now flowing down both arms.

On the horizon, a flash of light burst into the sky like a flare.

Like a beacon guiding her home.

Home to her dogs.

Home to herself.

To the home inside her own heart.

After a full day of floating on the open sea, the telltale currents of shore caught their raft, dragging them toward land. Their rugged scrap of wood collided with a rocky landmass not much bigger than one of the small islands in Arcadia's archipelago.

The waves that carried them in beat the wood against the rocky shore, destroying any hope they may have had to use the raft again.

They struggled through the rough surf and collapsed onto dry ground.

"How are you feeling?" Nora asked Cassian, who pushed himself up onto his feet, then pulled out their map.

The four Reds shook, flinging salt water into Nora and Cassian's faces.

He wiped his eyes, then touched the shirt he'd tied around his abdomen. A black liquid marked the area of the wound.

"Surprisingly, much better," he said. "The sleep helped." He paused. "And I've been thinking . . ."

"About?"

"The wound is just a scratch. Maybe I'll be okay."

"But you said the Bitter is in your blood."

"It is. But what if I'm immune?"

Nora tilted her head.

"I've been inflicted with the Bitter once before, then was treated by a healer. Perhaps that healing is still in effect."

Nora gave him a skeptical look.

"Honestly. I feel great."

"Great?" she asked.

"Well, okay . . . I feel good. I mean, I did just spend an entire day at sea on a scrap of wood. And I'm hungry."

At the mention of the word *hungry*, all four of the Reds snapped their heads in Cassian's direction. Their wide, pleading eyes blinked as they stared at him. Taran and Fable drooled.

"Hungry?" Taran said. "I'm hungry too."

Nora glanced around the dark shoreline, feeling her own stomach growl. It was definitely past their dinnertime. "Sorry." She patted Taran's head. "It doesn't look like we'll find much to eat here."

Taran's ears drooped.

"We'll figure something out," Cassian said. "But first, we need to find a way to get out there."

Nora followed the point of Cassian's finger to a rock formation that jutted from the sea not far off the shore where they stood.

"That big rock?" Nora asked.

Cassian unrolled the wet map. Thankfully, the waxy coating had preserved it well enough for them to make out the landmarks.

"Not just a rock," he said, pointing to the coordinates. "The landmass we're standing on is right here. But the *X* Orella drew is right there."

Nora traced the domed rock formation with her eyes. It was at least a couple hundred yards offshore, the size of a large building. She glanced down at the broken raft. The rough waves battered it against the rocks.

"So we . . . what? Swim out to it?" she asked.

"Got any better ideas?" Cassian asked.

Nora sighed. "Not really."

She recalled their journey up Mount Croia. "I'm sure it's going to be an unpleasant experience either way." She called her dogs to her side. "Rowan, Fable, come."

She crouched down when they reached her.

"I've had a lot of time to think today," she said. "And I've made a decision."

They stared at her with expectant eyes.

Her insides swirled as she said, "You two aren't going into the trove."

"What?" Rowan protested.

"Nora, this is a bad idea," Fable said.

She held up her hands to hold off their comments. "I've already made the decision."

She said it as much for herself as for them, reminding herself that she'd already processed all the possibilities and concluded this was the best option.

"Look, here's what I know: My emotions affect my bond with Rowan. In order to wield, I have to keep my energy in check." She paused. "And I can't do that if I'm worried about something happening to the two of you."

She swallowed, knowing she'd *still* be worried, but not nearly as fearful as she'd be if she brought them inside the trove. After seeing the horrifying dangers that lay at the top of Mount Croia, Nora knew there was no way she'd risk their lives at the next trove. Or risk her ability to wield, placing their entire group in danger as she'd done on the sailboat.

Rowan started to protest again. "But—"

"I need you to protect your brother," Nora said. "You were right. I should have listened to you back on the boat. You could have saved Fable. I didn't trust you then. But I'm trusting you now."

He sighed.

Nora glanced around the shore where they stood. "There's a lot of good cover here. Good places to hide." She pressed her lips together. "And although I can't guarantee it's safe . . ." Images of chimeras filled her mind. She quickly shoved them away. "I know it will be safer than if you go into the trove."

"But what about you?" Fable said.

She placed a hand on each of them. "I have my bond with Rowan. I know how to wield. And as long as I'm not distracted and fearing for your safety, I should be able to use the Eylan to overcome whatever it is I need to overcome in there."

Cassian, who'd been standing nearby, listening, asked, "Are you sure this is a good idea?"

She stood. "No. But it's the only way I know to protect them—to protect all of us—from me."

Cassian nodded, though his face said he didn't agree with the decision.

"But Rowan is the eidolon," Eira said.

"All the more reason to protect him," Nora added, remembering what Numair had said about him being a target. To Rowan, she said, "I trust you." She scratched behind his ear. "I trust you to protect yourself and your brother and to make the right choices for whatever the two of you may face." She swallowed against the tightness in her throat. "I love you both," she said, her tone filled with regret. She waded into the water, her own voice questioning her in her mind. "Stay, boys," she said.

They stared after her with sad, longing eyes.

Cassian joined her in the water. Taran and Eira waded out behind him.

"I'll be back soon," Nora called as she walked backward through the waves. They crashed against her ankles, then her knees.

"I promise I'll be back soon."

Eira and Taran had already begun their doggy paddle. Nora felt the ground drop beneath her. She could barely see the outline of her dogs on the darkened shore. But as she focused on her love for them, the visible cord of her bond with Rowan illuminated, connecting them and clearly guiding her way back to them.

"Stay," she commanded one last time, then ducked beneath the waves.

Nora, Cassian, Taran, and Eira bobbed in the waves beside the rocky landmass the map had indicated, already feeling exhausted. The formation was even bigger up close and soared above them like a large cathedral. They'd swum around it once, finding no way to come ashore or even climb the sheer rock walls that formed the towering domed structure.

"I may have found something," Eira finally said, doggy-paddling back toward the rest of their group from where she'd gone ahead to make a second lap.

They swam to catch up to her.

"Watch this," she said. She yipped, and ripples of Eylan danced in the water around her, then rushed forward directly toward the rock.

"There's a current," she said. "The water flows into the rock. I think there may be an entry point somewhere around here."

Nora treaded water, watching Eira's Eylan.

"So you're saying you think we need to go inside the rock?"

"I think so."

"Nice work," Cassian said. "I'll take a look." He ducked beneath the waves and popped up several seconds later, flicking his wet hair out of his eyes. "She's right. There's an underwater tunnel. We'll have to swim in."

Nora glanced back at the cord of Eylan that stretched all the way to the small island where she'd left her dogs. The fact that the bond still glowed thick and strong gave her the courage she needed. But it also left her feeling uneasy as she wondered what chimeras might be around to see it. She shoved the thought aside, not allowing it to pull her energy in the wrong direction. She needed to wield, and to wield, she needed her bond.

"I can wield air bubbles for all of us," she said.

"And I'll keep the water current illuminated so we can follow its direction," Eira added.

"Good idea," Nora said. Her eyes landed on Cassian. Though she couldn't see his torso, she pictured the torn shirt he still wore wrapped around his abdomen.

"You sure you're okay?" she asked him one last time.

"Yes," he said. "I'm as sure as the bond that stretches from you back to Rowan. Now wield us some air."

Nora hesitated, then nodded. She slowed the pace at which she treaded water, then fixed her mind on the sensation of her bond, not allowing her thoughts to drift to what might be swimming in the dark waters beneath them.

With a deep breath, she filled her lungs to make herself more buoyant, then kicked her legs harder to keep her head above water while she cupped her hands in front of her. When she pulled them apart, a sphere of Eylan stretched between her fingers. She expanded it until it was large enough to fit over Cassian's head, then placed it on him.

"Watching you wield never gets old," she heard his muffled voice say from inside the bubble. She quickly formed three more: one for Eira, Taran, and herself. The female Red ducked beneath the surface, leading the way with her elemental connection to the water.

Nora cast one final glance over her shoulder in the direction of her dogs, then followed.

They traveled straight into the rock, through a narrow underwater tunnel, following Eira's glowing currents until they reached a large inner cavern. Nora peered down through the dark blue, seeing an even deeper darkness that stretched below. It swallowed the light cast from Eira's Eylan, as if it had no bottom. A tingling sensation spread through her body at the sheer possibilities of the unknown. Nora felt grateful when another light reached them from above.

They followed the female Red as she swam up. Their heads broke the surface, bursting the air bubbles as they emerged inside the rock. Nora blinked and took in their surroundings.

Pristine-white coral covered the domed walls of a watery cave the size of a small gymnasium. Torches lit the perimeter, glimmering orange on the dark waters that stretched to fill the round chamber.

From where she bobbed near the edge, Nora could see a small round landmass in the center. Water surrounded it on all sides like a ring, and a white pillar towered on its center.

"The trove," Nora panted. "C'mon," she said, swimming toward it. The empty, bottomless feeling still tingled in her legs.

Cassian and the Reds followed.

They covered the distance and pulled themselves up onto the platform. Nora immediately rolled over and collapsed onto her back, grateful for a moment to catch her breath. And even more grateful to be out of the water. Cassian flopped down beside her.

Bleached coral covered the surface beneath her as well as the marble pillar that towered in its center. From where Nora lay, she could see the torches that hung in stands around the thick column, illuminating the stunning structure that stretched all the way to the ceiling.

Nora pushed herself up and stood. Water dripped from her soaked clothes. She started to turn to offer Cassian a hand up, then froze. Four large copper bowls surrounded the column, imbedded in the coral platform. A Red lay in each bowl.

She rushed to the nearest dog. The female lifted her head to look at Nora, reminding her of when she'd found Fable at the first trove. A sour feeling swelled in Nora's gut.

"Oh no," she heard Cassian say from behind her. "This is bad."

Nora scanned the platform until she found what she was looking for. A small white pedestal sat beside the giant pillar. She stood and crossed over to it to find a foot-wide circular imprint with a coin-sized circular reservoir in its center, filled with a golden liquid, just as they'd found at the first trove.

She touched the cool marble of the pedestal's surface, careful to avoid the well of power in its center, remembering that the liquid connected directly to the entire store of Eylan in the trove.

They'd need an aureus to unleash it.

A soft whimper drew her attention. She followed the sound around to the back of the pillar where a fifth copper bowl nestled in the coral surface.

Nora's hand flew to cover her mouth. She dropped to her knees. A tiny pup curled in the bottom of the bowl, shivering, a long wormlike tube attached to his pink belly.

Rowan paced back and forth along the rocky shore, knowing he and Fable should find a good spot to hide as Nora had suggested, yet he was unable to look away from the rock in the distance and the long, glowing cord of Eylan that stretched toward it.

"Staying is torture," he mumbled. "What if she needs us right now?"

Fable said nothing but stood in the shallow of the water, nose sniffing the air. Finally he said, "I've lost her scent."

Rowan stopped pacing. "This isn't good." He uttered a soft whine, then came to stand beside his brother. They watched in silence as the waves crashed around their paws.

He inched closer, feeling the palpable warmth of Fable's presence. He lingered in his brother's energy, soaking it in. He'd missed it terribly in the days following Fable's passing from the Kingdom of Kentucky.

Rowan recalled that moment in the kitchen when he'd felt the swell of his brother's energy right before it had vanished.

He'd thought he'd never feel it again.

Thought he'd never see Fable again.

He turned his head to stare at his brother.

He found himself staring often, as if to make sure he was still there.

Fable *was* there.

But he was also different.

And so was Rowan.

He was an eidolon now.

Many things felt different after that surge of power had rushed into his body.

His senses felt heightened.

His instincts more intense.

His love for Nora and Fable had deepened as well.

As had his sense of duty to protect them.

It felt more urgent, more necessary.

But one thing hadn't changed.

Rowan still had his brother.

He smiled, despite his concern for Nora.

"The bond is still visible," Rowan finally said. "So that must mean she's okay, right?"

Fable was silent for a long moment before he said solemnly, "You and I will always see the bond. Even if she can't see it. Even if she isn't okay."

Rowan nudged his brother's cheek with his nose as he'd done since he was a pup.

"I'm glad to be with you again," Rowan said. "Like this. It was . . . different after you passed."

"I know," Fable said. "But Coeur needed help."

Rowan leaned against his brother. "And now Nora needs our help. So what do we do? Just . . . *stay*?"

Fable pawed at the waves. "No. I don't think that's what she *really* wanted. Right?"

Rowan snapped his head to look at his brother. "I was thinking the same thing! I mean, it's just like when we were back in the Kingdom of Kentucky. She would go across the field to the barn but tell us to stay by the house. She never really meant it. And we always followed her anyway."

"It made her laugh," Fable said.

"I love making her laugh!" Rowan added, thinking of how he'd licked the tears from her face in the days following Fable's passing, tickling her cheeks until she finally gave in with a soft smile. "She's my best friend."

"Mine too," Fable said.

"She's our human."

Fable nodded. "And that's why we can be certain she didn't really mean it when she told us to stay."

"Agreed!" Rowan released a gleeful bark and trotted deeper into the water, Fable at his side.

They waded out until their feet couldn't touch, as they'd done countless times in the pond back on the farm in Kentucky. Then, following the glowing Eylan Bond that stretched across the ocean, they doggy-paddled toward their human.

CHAPTER ELEVEN

NORA RUSHED FROM DOG TO DOG, checking on each of the other four Reds who lay inside the copper bowls. Each had a similar tube attached to its belly.

"I need your help," she said to Cassian. "We have to detach these tubes."

"What are they?" he asked, stooping next to an adult male.

"I don't know," Nora grunted, pulling one from the female she'd first seen. She held up the tube to examine the strange sucker attachment on the end. It almost looked alive. "Gross." She tossed it to the side. "It must have something to do with the way Queen Kierra's siphoning their power into the trove. It doesn't matter, though. We're getting these dogs out of here."

"How?" Eira asked as she checked on one of the adult Reds. "They're so weak. And we have no boat."

Nora returned to the pup. "I don't know," she said. "But we can't leave them here. We'll find a way to get them out, take them to Rowan and Fable, then come back."

"What about the aureus?" Taran asked. "We need to find it so we can unleash the Eylan."

Nora lifted the frail pup. He looked to be no more than two months old. And he was so thin. She cradled him in her arms and started to remove the tube from his belly.

He yelped in pain.

"Shh . . . I'm sorry," she said into his ear. "I have to remove it. It's making you sick." She gave him a moment to settle. "I haven't seen the aureus," she replied to Taran, then thought back to the first trove. "I'm almost afraid to know where it is."

"That's the last one," she heard Cassian say as he pulled a tube from another male Red's abdomen. He lifted the appendage to examine the sucker on the end. "Strange," he muttered.

"You ready?" Nora asked the pup.

He stared up at her with wide golden eyes—eyes like Fable's. In fact, he looked a lot like Fable when he was a puppy.

She cradled him against her chest. "Okay, here we go. Like ripping off a bandage."

"Uh, Nora?"

She ignored Cassian, focusing her attention on the sickly pup.

"One," she said, gripping the tube.

"Nora."

"Two." She ensured she had a good grip on the slippery material.

"Nora!"

"Three!"

She ripped the tube from the pink skin of the pup's belly.

He howled in pain.

"Nora!" Cassian shouted again.

"What?"

She spun to see him standing at the edge of the coral platform, still holding the strange tube.

The pup whimpered in her arms.

Cassian lifted the tube into the air, demonstrating how its length disappeared over the edge of the platform and into the inky waters.

A suctioning sound slurped near Nora's ear. She looked down to see the tube she still held in one hand. The sucker attachment pinched open and closed.

Like a mouth.

Nora shrieked and dropped it, watching as the tube slithered toward the water, then retreated under the surface.

The water around the platform rippled.

Then writhed.

Bubbles formed along the surface.

"Get away from the edge!" Nora shouted at Cassian. She clutched the pup to her chest. "Eira, Taran, come!" she commanded.

The Reds ran to her side. Nora stepped in front of them, keeping them between her and the coral-coated marble pillar in the center of the platform. She could feel the hum of Eylan radiating from it. She glanced at the small pedestal with the well of liquid gold. She could stick her finger in it and directly access the Eylan of the trove. But she knew that without Rowan physically present to channel and wield the Eylan like the last time, she wouldn't be able to withstand the power.

Cassian stood beside her, pressing his shoulder against hers. She glanced at the makeshift bandage around his middle. The black stain of his wound somehow seemed worse.

"I really wish you had your bow and arrow right now," Nora said.

"Even if I hadn't lost it in the shipwreck, it would've been a little hard to swim with it."

Nora heard a rasp from the female Red who still lay in the copper bowl. "Get . . . out of . . . here," she wheezed.

Nora glanced around the circular platform. The four adult Reds curled in their copper bowls, shivering. The pup she held trembled.

The surface of the water erupted. A giant form rose from the depths.

Nora recognized the bulbous head of a giant octopus. Dozens of unblinking yellow eyes covered its slippery skin in vertical rows, interspersed with countless razor-tipped horns. Two massive tentacles rose in front of it, parting to reveal a circular mouth lined with concentric rings of glistening teeth, like a deadly bull's-eye leading all the way to the back of its throat. The monster released a shrill roar.

To the right of its gigantic head, two more tentacles surfaced, each one lined with the writhing tubes they'd found attached to the Reds. They rippled as if reaching for them. Another tentacle surfaced behind the monster's enormous head.

Nora froze.

A red rope was tied to the appendage, and on it, a twelve-inch-wide gold medallion.

"The aureus," she breathed.

"You've got to be kidding me," Cassian said. "What do we do?"

Nora's mind raced through every lesson she'd learned from Numair. But in the moment, her brain couldn't think of any way she might use Rowan's elemental power of air to get the aureus.

"Eira, Taran, any ideas?" Nora asked, gripping tightly to the pup. "A water tornado maybe, or a—"

One of the tentacles struck Nora, flinging her backward into the coral-covered column where her head hit with a sickening thud.

She heard the pup whimper in her arms. Heard Cassian scream. Eira bark. Taran yelp.

And then everything went black, even the glowing bond between her and Rowan.

Nora groaned and rolled to her side. When she opened her eyes, a blurry vision of the white cavern greeted her. She blinked the world into focus.

Cassian lay on the other side of the platform, unconscious. Wriggling tubes suctioned the wound on his abdomen. Eira and Taran were curled up beside him, appearing as dazed as Nora felt.

She started to crawl toward Cassian, to rip the tubes from his belly.

"Don't," a voice said in a harsh whisper.

Nora turned. It was the female Red who'd warned them to run. The weak dog lifted her head but couldn't move from her place in the copper bowl. "Don't disturb it while it's feeding. Come," the dog said. "Come closer."

"Feeding?" Nora's stomach flipped.

She touched the back of her head, feeling a hot, sticky liquid. When she pulled her hand away, blood coated her fingers. Turning to look at the coral-studded column where she'd hit her head, she saw that it, too, was stained red.

Nora pulled herself along the white floating platform toward the female Red, her eyes scanning the surrounding water for the trove monster. Other than the suctioning tubes that had attached themselves to Cassian, there was no sign of it.

"Stay far away from the edge," the female Red cautioned as Nora inched closer.

"Who are you?" Nora asked.

"My name is Lumi," she said. "Who are you? And more importantly, why have you come to this wretched place?"

"My name is Nora. I'm here to save you. And to unleash the Eylan here at this trove."

Lumi scanned Nora with heavy eyes. "It's *you.*"

Nora nodded.

"And are *they* with you?" she asked.

"The boy and the two Reds? Yes. Which is why I need to help him—"

"No, not them. *Them.*" Lumi used what little strength she had to point with her nose.

Nora rose up on her knees and looked out across the floating coral platform, across the ring of water that surrounded it, to see two dogs swimming toward her.

Nora's dogs.

"Get out of the water!" she said in a loud whisper.

Rowan and Fable doggy-paddled toward her and pulled themselves up onto the platform with their front paws.

"Hi, Nora!" Rowan said, his voice echoing through the cavern.

"Shh, keep your voice down."

"Oh no!" Fable said in a low voice. "What happened to Cassian?"

"I don't have a lot of time to explain, but—" She stopped and stared at her two dogs for a long moment, shook her head, then said, "You two were never very good at *stay*."

"You said you trusted me to make the right choices while you were gone," Rowan said, tongue flopping from one side of his mouth. "This was the right choice!" He licked her hand, then added, "We followed the bond, but it winked out when we were swimming through the tunnel. Are you all right?"

Nora touched the wound on the back of her head. "I was unconscious. I'm okay now, but Cassian . . . We need to pull those things off him. Then get the aureus, which is tied to a monster beneath the water."

"How do we do that?" Fable asked.

"I can help," a small voice said.

Nora turned to see the tiny, sickly pup waddle toward her from the other side of the coral column, stumbling on unsteady feet.

"There you are." She picked him up, feeling his thin, bony body.

Cassian groaned. She rushed to his side, then set the pup down.

"What's happening to me?" he asked, reaching for the tubes that writhed from the opening in his abdomen.

"Don't touch them," Nora cautioned. "We're going to get them off of you, but we can't disturb the creature while it's . . . feeding."

"Feeding?" Cassian reached to yank one out.

"Just wait," Nora said. "Rowan's here. Fable too. We're going to figure something out."

"I can help," the pup said again in a weak voice.

Nora eyed him nose to tail. He couldn't have weighed more than twelve pounds. Cassian turned his head to look at the tiny Red. His eyes sparked with recognition. Nora stroked a hand over the pup's head. "You Reds amaze me, always so eager to help, even when it's dangerous." She didn't have the heart to tell him that he was far too little and sick to be of any real help. Instead, she said, "You should save your energy. You're going to need it once we figure out a way to get the aureus and get out of here."

He uttered a soft whimper. "But I know what to do," he said.

Nora titled her head to one side.

The puppy sniffed Cassian. "The Bitter is in the blood."

"The Bitter is in the blood?" Nora repeated.

"Yes. And the Bitter is flammable." The pup planted his front paws on Cassian's rib cage so he could better see the wound and the tubes that emerged from it. "There's Bitter in his blood, and the monster is drinking it."

Nora's stomach turned. "Is that what it was doing to you and the other dogs?"

The puppy coughed. "No. Our blood is still red. But the monster doesn't care what color our blood is."

"It can't pass the Bitter through the tubes," one of the other Reds weakly added. "But it can through its bite."

Nora recalled the circles of jagged teeth she'd seen.

"Okay," she said, turning her attention back to the pup. "The Bitter is in the blood. So what do you suggest we do?"

The pup looked up at her with his wide golden eyes. "We have to burn the Bitter."

"Burn it?"

"I think I see where he's going with this," Cassian grunted, pushing up onto his elbows. He sighed. "Come here," he said to Nora.

She knelt beside him.

"There is Bitter in my blood. There is also Bitter in this creature's blood."

"Right."

"And it's currently feeding on me."

Nora shivered. "I know, but I don't understand what this has to do with—"

"You must ignite my wound."

"What?"

"The Bitter in my wound will catch flame, then pass into the creature as it feeds."

Nora stood and backed away, shaking her head. "No. No, I won't do that. First, it makes no sense."

"It makes perfect sense," Cassian said. "We have to do something."

"And that something is to kill you?"

"No," the pup said. "It won't kill him. I won't let it."

Again, Nora shook her head. "How? How can you do that?"

"His elemental power is fire," Cassian said.

Nora stared down at him. "What? How do you know—"

"I recognize him now," Cassian said. "This is Princess Sadie's pup."

Fable's ears lifted. He rushed over and sniffed the tiny golden. "It's you!"

"The pup that went missing," Nora said.

"Yes. And he's right," Cassian said through a groan. "This is the only way."

"But he's a puppy," Nora protested.

"What does his age have to do with anything?" Cassian asked.

"Not his age . . . his experience, his skill."

"Wielding is instinctual for Reds," Rowan said. "Remember?"

Nora softened. "Yes, it's just—"

"If I keep the flame flowing in one direction, it won't burn him," the pup said. "Not much, at least."

"Then why not just burn its tentacle or these tubes? Why risk burning Cassian at all?"

"Because we need to ignite the Bitter," Cassian said. "Not the monster's flesh. We need to ignite the liquid so the flame travels through its entire body."

"Like igniting oil," Nora mumbled. "Or gasoline."

"It will make it angry," the pup said. "Then you can grab the aureus." He panted, weary just from speaking.

Nora's chest rose with a deep breath. "This is still a terrible idea."

The pup sat on his bony rump and huffed a whimper. "I can do it. I can help. You just have to trust me."

"I trust him!" Rowan said.

"He's Sadie's pup," Fable said. "A brother. I trust him too!"

"Eira, grab one of those torches," Cassian said.

Before Nora had time to protest again or command otherwise, Eira crossed the small platform to the center where the white coral pillar towered. She rose up on her hind paws and carefully removed the torch from its stand using her teeth. She retrieved it and brought it to Nora.

"Now, listen to me," Cassian said as he motioned for Nora to crouch beside him. "You're going to touch this flame to my wound, and the Bitter will ignite in my blood. It will burn, but it will not set me ablaze."

Nora swallowed. "I can't do this."

"You can," Cassian said.

"Okay, maybe I *can* do this, but I *won't* do this."

"You will," he said. "Because you are Nora the Bonded, the Whole One, the girl who will save us all." He held her stare. "The girl who made her home in Coeur," he added. "This is *your* kingdom, Nora. And only you can save it."

Reaching for her hand that held the torch, Cassian guided the flame toward the open wound on his abdomen. "Trust the pup. Rowan and Fable trust him. And you trust them."

Nora felt like she was watching from a distance as Cassian guided the torch closer, like watching a movie. She couldn't believe she was about to set her friend's blood on fire.

She blinked.

Her friend.

"One last thing," Cassian said. "If this doesn't work, it has been my great honor to know you, Nora."

"If this *doesn't* work? But you said—"

"And if it *does* work," Cassian interrupted, "then I'm really going to need a healer after this."

Before she could say anything, Cassian yanked her hand and touched the flame to his open wound.

His scream echoed through the cavern.

Nora jumped to her feet, activating her bond with Rowan. The cord of liquid-light blazed vibrantly between them, wrapping Rowan's chest in a glowing shield and Nora's left arm in a sleeve of light. They all watched the monster's parasitic tubes writhe as the fire traveled invisibly beneath the surface of its skin.

The water bubbled as if boiling, and the creature's bulbous head reappeared, its many eyes staring in their direction.

Nora glanced at Sadie's pup, the strain evident on his tiny face as the flames licked his fur but didn't burn him. "I . . . can do . . . this," he grunted. "Get . . . the . . . aureus."

Rowan jumped into action. Eira and Taran raced on his heels.

The monster roared as if in pain, opening its tentacles wide, revealing the fanged bull's-eye of its mouth.

Eight tentacles emerged from the inky depths, each lined with the familiar sucker-tipped tubes.

Torchlight glinted on the monster's wet body.

And on the aureus.

"There it is!" Nora shouted.

Taran struck first, howling until the roof of the cave trembled. Shards of the white coral broke away in jagged pieces and crashed into the monster's head.

But the attack only angered it.

A flash of movement caught Nora's peripheral vision. Without thinking, she shoved her hands forward and released an air pulse. She struck one of the monster's tentacles.

The appendage lurched away from her attack, revealing a footlong hooked claw on the tip of the tentacle. Nora didn't know if the creature could inflict the Bitter with its claws, too, but she wasn't about to find out.

Eira released a rapid staccato of barks, sending the waters around the platform spiraling, forcing the monster to spin with them, bringing its back tentacles closer.

Cassian's wails backdropped the chaos.

Nora tried to shove them from her awareness and fixed her attention on the coursing bond between her and Rowan.

The monster's eyes bulged as its insides boiled.

Taran continued to shower the monster with raining shards of coral, disorienting it as it slapped its massive tentacles along the surface of the water, as if it could slow Eira's whirlpool.

Nora could feel the temperature of the cavern rise as the monster's body boiled from the inside.

"It's flammable," she mumbled while wielding another pulse to fling a talon-tipped tentacle away from Cassian. "Which means it's combustible."

Smoke curled from two holes near the monster's mouth—its nostrils.

Nora's eyes widened. "It's going to blow," she said. Then louder, "Guys! We need to get the aureus and get out of here! That thing is going to explode!"

"She's right!" Eira shouted.

Cassian had gone silent.

Rowan barked his own air pulse, deflecting a tentacle from Fable, who stood near the smaller pillar, examining the divot of liquid-light—the connection point for the aureus.

"I have an idea," Fable said. "Rowan, give me a lift!"

Rowan turned to face his brother. Nora watched the unspoken communication pass between them, then Rowan gave a nod. "Fetch!" he shouted.

The muscles in Fable's hindquarters bunched as he crouched. Then he took off.

"Fable, no!"

But Nora didn't have time to allow her fear to seep through the bond. Fable sprinted across the platform as Rowan howled. Liquid-light rippled from his mouth, forming currents of air that lifted Fable as he leapt.

He landed on top of the creature's head.

"Fable!"

But he didn't stop.

The monster spun through the water, caught in Eira's current. It flailed its massive tentacles, trying to cease its spin. One slammed into the cavern wall, causing even more shards of coral to rain down.

Fable leapt from the monster's head to the nearest tentacle.

"A little help, brother!" he shouted to Rowan.

"Don't be afraid, Nora," Rowan said. "Keep our bond strong. Trust us!"

"I trust you," she said with trembling lips. "I trust you." She wielded again as one of the other tentacles nearly slammed down on the four Reds, who watched helplessly from their copper bowls.

"Watch out for the claws!" Nora shouted.

Rowan barked and howled and yipped, controlling the currents of air as Fable leapt from one tentacle to another, as if he were jumping to catch a Frisbee.

Finally, he reached the one that held the aureus.

Nora watched as her beloved dog grasped the red rope between his teeth and pulled.

A pulse rippled through the monster.

It jerked, nearly throwing Fable.

"We're out of time!" Eira shouted. "It's going to blow now!"

"No," Nora said under her breath. Not when Fable was on top of it. Not when they were this close.

Fable finally ripped the aureus from the creature's tentacle, then began leaping his way back toward them.

The monster lurched again.

Nora felt her energy begin to sink with her dread, pulling her downward.

But something Rowan had said stuck in her mind.

"There is a way to leap in fear and a way to leap in love."

Like Fable did now.

She wouldn't allow her fear to drag him down. Not again. She'd lift him as Rowan did.

Nora touched a hand to her chest, feeling the ripple of energy that pulsed there—the Eylan. She closed her eyes, focusing all her attention on the bond, on the power Rowan shared with her—on the aureus he wore around his neck.

A jolt of energy surged up the bond and alighted in her chest. She felt the eidolon's familiar power.

When she opened her eyes, the monster continued to seethe in front of her, but now Nora knew what to do.

"Thank you, science class," she said, then arced her arms, creating multiple glowing pockets of air at once. They descended upon her, Cassian, and the Reds.

"Breathe!" she commanded as the air pockets surrounded their heads. And though she'd never done it in practice with Numair, Nora thrust a hand into the air, fingers splayed. With all the instinct of a Red, she clenched her fingers into a fist. A suctioning sound filled the cavern, and the air inside vanished.

The sea monster flailed, but Nora no longer feared its combustion.

It couldn't explode if there was no oxygen.

But the Bitter could still burn on the inside.

The chimera flailed all eight of its tentacles at once, throwing Fable's body across the cavern.

Nora gasped.

The aureus fell from his mouth as his body sailed across the cavern. The gold medallion clanged against the platform where Nora and the other Reds stood. But she didn't move toward it, instead sprinting in Fable's direction. He yelped as his body hit the cavern wall, then slipped into the water.

"Eira! Help!" Nora commanded from inside her bubble. She rushed to the edge of the platform and dropped to her knees, eyes searching the water.

"I'll get Fable!" Eira said. She appeared at Nora's side. "You get the aureus!"

A tentacle slammed the platform, hitting Cassian and throwing Sadie's pup to the side with a loud whimper.

"Go get the aureus!" Eira commanded again, then wielded the waters with her barks, commanding them to cease their spiral and instead rise.

"I'm not going anywhere!" Nora said as she leaned into her bond with Rowan, tapping into the potent eidolon power to command the air pocket around Fable's body to lift.

Rowan and Taran howled, continuing to wield their Eylan against the monster as Eira and Nora fought to save Fable.

Her frantic eyes scanned the water, searching for

her dog. But just as she readied herself to dive in after him, a dark form rose through the water.

Fable's body lifted on top of it.

Two large wide-set eyes appeared through the dark waters, then blinked.

Nora and Eira stumbled back from the edge.

A chimera—part whale, part manta ray—breached the surface, only a portion of its gigantic kite-shaped body visible. It wore a large contraption around its torso, made of leather straps that reminded Nora of Arcturus's harness. A smaller strap encircled its dorsal fin, affixed with a metal emblem. Nora instantly recognized the intricate mandala design, the same crest Arcturus had worn.

"I'm a friend," the creature blubbed. "Sent by Orella. We must leave. And quickly."

"But Fable," Nora said, unable to pull her stare from her dog, who sprawled on the creature's back.

"He's okay," the chimera said. "I have him."

"Nora!" Eira shouted through her own air pocket. "Go get the—"

A shock of energy exploded through the cavern.

Nora fell to the platform and turned to see Sadie's tiny pup standing on top of the smaller pillar where he'd placed the aureus, his little paw pressed against its golden surface. Eylan shot upward around the edges in a column of liquid-light.

Then the puppy collapsed.

"No!" Nora sprinted toward him. "Rowan, help me!" she commanded. "Get everyone on . . . him." She pointed toward the whalelike creature—the trove guardian.

She snatched up Sadie's pup and the now coin-sized aureus that bore his little pawprint. "I can't believe it," she uttered. She flipped the medallion over, seeing the same intricate mandala that etched Rowan's aureus imprinted on the opposite side of the golden disc.

She stood there, shocked, clutching the panting pup, while Eira, Taran, and Rowan assisted the other Reds, Rowan levitating their bodies a few inches from their copper bowls while Eira and Taran dragged them toward the trove guardian.

Nora carried the pup over, entrusting him and the aureus to Rowan. She checked to see that Fable was breathing inside his pocket of air, then returned for Cassian.

A violent gash marred his thigh where black liquid leaked. The monster had torn his leg open with one of its claws.

Hungry tentacles reached for them. The beast flashed its teeth.

Hooking her arms under Cassian's, Nora released her hold on the surrounding air, allowing oxygen to once again fill the chamber. With all the force of her bond, she dragged Cassian to the edge of the platform and onto the trove guardian's back, watching as the tentacled monster across the cavern seethed with rage and burning Bitter. She quickly ensured all the Reds still had their air pockets to allow them to breathe, checked that everyone was securely strapped in, then commanded the trove guardian to dive.

Mere seconds into their descent, Nora felt the shock of the explosion.

An unexpected wave of grief hit her as the detonation rippled through the water. She pictured the monster inside the trove, imagining the beautiful creature it once was—before Queen Kierra had poisoned it with her Bitter.

From inside the safety of her air pocket, Nora chanted, "Come, Eylan, on eternal wings. Imbue this vessel, as Mother sings. Embrace transition to endless grace. Return to source and divine embrace."

A flash of light flickered through the serene blue that enveloped them. The trove guardian continued its descent, carrying them down and down into a much deeper passage that cut through the cavern, then out into the open sea.

Moments later, they crested the surface.

The air pockets they wore burst like sudsy bubbles, and everyone sucked in deep breaths of salty air.

Nora scanned her pack.

Everyone remained strapped to the trove guardian, soaking wet and wearing weary expressions. The four new adult Reds they'd recovered appeared incredibly weak but looked like they would survive. Rowan, Taran, and Eira wore fatigued expressions but seemed otherwise okay.

"Fable?" she asked, seeing him pant. "Are you all right?"

"I'll be okay," he said. "Just some scratches and bruises from the coral."

She nodded.

But her eyes fell on Cassian.

Then Sadie's pup.

She spoke to the trove guardian. "You said you know Orella? You're a Rebel?"

"Yes, my name is Osias. And I've been stationed here with the instruction that if anyone should ever unleash the Eylan at this trove, I must take them to meet the oracle Sivilla, who lives in the jungles of Eblor."

Without taking her eyes off Cassian and the sickly pup who curled beside him, she said, "Good, but first we need to make a stop in Yarou. I need to get this pup to his mother and my friend to a healer."

CHAPTER TWELVE

WITH OSIAS'S SPEED AND EIRA'S manipulation of the ocean currents, it took the trove guardian only a day to reach the southernmost inlet at the border between Oorbara and Yarou. From there, Osias said it would take another half day to travel up the river and reach the lake near the Reds' hidden home. Still, Nora had urged him to hurry. One glance at Cassian was enough to tell her they were running out of time.

The chimera's massive watery wingspan carried them along the surface of the waves, his back wide and long enough to hold all eleven of them. But even with his impressive size, it was impossible to stay dry. Nora longed to slip into some clean clothes, to don a fresh pair of socks. She hadn't been dry since before their shipwreck, and that had been over two days ago.

They were hungry.

And thirsty.

So thirsty.

But the Eylan preserved them.

Everyone except Cassian.

With every passing minute, Nora feared he wouldn't make it.

Despite the warmth of the afternoon southern sun, a distinct chill settled over everyone, worst for Sadie's pup. His frail body shivered from the constant wet, and though he breathed at a normal pace, his eyes had remained closed since they'd fled the trove.

Nora pulled him to her chest, cradling him in her arms. She glanced down at the gold aureus she'd tied around his neck with the red rope. His tiny pawprint glimmered up at her.

"Is it possible?" she asked Eira, who sat beside her. "Is it possible for him to be an eidolon?"

"Not just possible," Eira said. "It's true. When he touched the aureus, the Eylan chose him to be a priest, just as it chose Rowan."

"All the more reason to get him to Sadie, then," Nora said.

Eira sniffed the pup. "His actions were honorable. He saved us all. And right now, I suspect those actions are the only thing saving Cassian."

"What do you mean?"

"I'm no healer," Eira said, "but the fire seems to have cauterized Cassian's initial wound, slowing the spread of the Bitter."

"But what about his leg?" Nora asked, pointing to the necrotic web that surrounded the gash in his thigh. "I guess the trove monster's claw also had the poison?"

Eira lowered her head. "It seems so. Which could mean he'll succumb anyway."

Cassian mumbled as if in a fitful sleep. The wound on his thigh, visible through the tear in his pants, continued to darken with the Bitter that seeped into his veins.

Nora couldn't be certain, but the skin surrounding both wounds appeared different, and not just in color. The texture was all wrong—slippery around his abdomen, bumpy on his leg.

She sighed, cradled the pup tighter, then turned to check on everyone else.

The four adult Reds they'd rescued remained strapped in place, too weary to stand and remain steady during the bumpy ride.

Taran sat in the middle of them, keeping close watch. He'd already confirmed that none of them were healers. Even if they were, they were far too weak to wield.

Nora noticed Rowan and Fable, who sat toward the rear, side by side, facing backward, leaning close to one another as if in deep conversation.

The pup whimpered, then shivered.

"I'm worried about him," Nora said, stroking the soft fur on the wide bridge of his nose.

"Yes, he's quite sick," Eira said. "They all are. Though I fear Cassian is the worst."

"I wish I could do something."

"You are," Eira said. "You're wise to take him and the Reds to Sadie. Especially her pup. She'll be overjoyed to be reunited with him."

"I can imagine," Nora said, thinking of the overwhelming gratitude she still felt at being reunited with Fable.

He turned to face her from the back, as if he'd felt her stare, as if he'd heard her thoughts.

"More than you can imagine," Eira said. "Sadie lost a brother when she was just a pup—her beloved brother, her best friend. His disappearance impacted her deeply."

"What happened?" Nora asked.

"He went missing during a family pilgrimage to the Temple of Eylan. He was older than this pup but still quite young." Eira's ears lowered. Her eyes held a deep sadness. "When Sadie's pup went missing it brought much of that pain to the surface."

Nora nodded somberly.

Eira watched her for a long moment before speaking again. "You love Fable dearly."

"Yes," Nora said.

"And Rowan too," Eira added.

He turned, hearing his name.

"Yes, of course," Nora said, seeing Rowan's smile, noting the gold aureus around his neck. "They're my world, my everything, my . . . my heart."

Eira nodded knowingly. "There is no limit to love, you know. There is always more to be had, more to be shared. And it has no end. It never dies, only changes form."

Nora furrowed her brow, hearing the familiar phrase.

"I heard what Orella said to you before leaving Arcadia," Eira added. "She was right. It's time for you to learn to live and love again."

Nora swallowed, thinking of her journey through Coeur, thinking of all she'd been through since that moment Fable had collapsed in her kitchen. "How?" she asked. "How do I live and love when I'm terrified that the ones I love most will be ripped from me?"

Eira held her gaze with deep, compassionate eyes. "Ah yes, that was why you made Rowan and Fable stay back when we went inside the trove."

Nora nodded. "To protect them. I did it out of love."

Eira shook her head. "You did it out of fear. Compounded fear, actually—a fear of feeling fear."

Nora opened her mouth to protest, then closed it, realizing Eira was right. "My first lesson with the Eylan . . . You told me love and fear are often confused."

"Yes," Eira said. "But there is a very easy way to tell the difference."

"What's that?"

"Fear is most easily identified by clinging—hoarding—like Kierra hoards the Eylan. Love is about letting go—flowing—allowing the Eylan to flow from you to another, not knowing if it will return but trusting and believing that it will."

Eira's words blurred in Nora's mind.

"Make sense?" the female Red asked.

Nora shook her head. "I think I'm just . . . tired. And hungry and thirsty and ready to be back on dry land."

"Aren't we all?" Eira chuckled. "But may I make a simple suggestion for how you might begin to live and love again?"

"Sure."

"The pup." Eira nudged the tiny Red in Nora's arms. "Start with him. He is very weak. And your love can help sustain him."

Nora stroked his little head. "I do love him."

"No, *truly* love him. Love him like you love them." She nodded in the direction of Rowan and Fable. "Give yourself to him fully, all while knowing his time in this realm may be short. While knowing he could break your heart."

Nora bit her bottom lip. Tears pooled in her eyes. They spilled over when she glanced in Fable's direction.

"It's okay to grieve, Nora. Grief is an expression of love. Just be careful not to allow fear to taint it." She paused, her tone shifting. "And remember, once a bond forms, it's always there. Even when you can't see it. Even when you can't feel it. Love can still flow because the bond still exists."

Nora hugged the pup closer, nodding, thinking of how she'd experienced that very thing with Rowan. But the tone of Eira's voice hinted at something deeper.

"You should name him," Eira said.

"Doesn't he already have a name?" Nora asked.

"Princess Sadie always waited to name her pups until after she'd weaned them. He was taken from his mother far too early." Eira's tone shifted to one of sadness. "He's missed so much."

Nora hugged the thin pup closer and nuzzled her face against the top of his head. He uttered a soft sigh.

She couldn't believe this tiny Red had saved all of them back at the trove. And yet, he had. He was truly worthy of the title he now bore—Eidolon of Coeur.

"Honor," Nora whispered. "Your name is Honor."

Nora roused Cassian as soon as they reached Yarou Lake. Using scraps of fabric torn from the hem of her tunic, she made a sling to carry Honor, then helped Cassian to shore where they found sticks to splint his leg. Rowan, Fable, Eira, and Taran helped the four other Reds disembark. Osias promised to wait for Nora so he could take her and her dogs to meet the next oracle after dropping off Cassian and the sickly Reds.

With the help of Nora's supporting arm, Cassian pushed through his delirium to make the trek from the lake to the woods, then through the ravine that Nora recognized from when she'd first arrived in Coeur. Eira and Taran took the lead, guiding them into a cavern opening and through familiar winding underground tunnels until they emerged in the canyon where Cassian had first brought Nora and Rowan.

"Home," Eira breathed as they stepped out of the cave.

Nora took in the view of the wide circular canyon and the towering stone walls that edged them in. For the first time in weeks, she felt safe, knowing the towering evergreen sentries watched over and hid them.

Weeks.

She'd been in Coeur for nearly *three* weeks.

The thought jolted her.

But before she had time to ruminate on her absence from Earth, she focused her attention on the task at hand.

She had to get Cassian and their new Red friends to a healer.

The pine trees spread their boughs like welcoming arms and beckoned them forward up the sloping hill and into the Reds' home, where the midday sun seeped through to the forest floor.

Nora steadied herself beneath Cassian's weight and began leading him.

Taran trotted ahead, tail wagging, then froze. His tail stiffened.

"What is it?" Nora asked.

He lifted his nose to the air. "I smell . . . smoke."

"Smoke?" Alarm hinted in Cassian's voice.

Both Taran and Eira sprinted up the sloped earth, through the pines, and toward the dogs' dens. Rowan and Fable followed.

Nora helped Cassian up the incline. When they reached the top, a sorrowful howl pierced the air.

Taran and Eira stood in the center of their home, faces turned toward the sky, releasing mournful cries.

Charred earth surrounded them.

The entire pack was gone.

CHAPTER THIRTEEN

QUEEN KIERRA DESCENDED THE WINDING spiral staircase into the bowels of her castle. The scent of damp stone greeted her, along with the flicker of torchlight. She navigated the slick steps carefully, placing her taloned eagle foot firmly on the treads to support her uneven gait. But the heeled shoe she wore on her human foot still managed to slip. She caught herself on the rail before she could fall, cursed her cumbersome body under her breath, then pushed a stray strand of hair from her face. She huffed and continued making her way to the bottom.

A dank, darkened corridor stretched in front of her, lined with prison cells, all of them filled with Reds and the other dogs she'd captured from Yarou. It had been a while since the dungeons had been occupied. Kierra rarely used them anymore, finding the threat of prison to be less effective at controlling her subjects than the promise of a reward. Which was why, when she needed to dispose of a subject—like Thorne—she housed them in the western wing of the castle and bestowed upon them riches and delicacies. She plumped them up with food and wine, dazzled them with luxury, allowing the rumors of the kingdom's wonderful queen to spread. Then when the moment was right, the subject would just . . . disappear. Reassigned to another territory, or at least that's what her subjects assumed.

They never suspected they went to visit the ammit.

Of course, Kierra also wielded the threat of the ammit as needed. But she was careful not to let her court realize that the fanged beast was the punishment *and* the prize.

She paused to peer through one of the barred doors, seeing four unconscious dogs curled together, collars of viscous Bitter wrapped around their necks to ensure they couldn't wield. She moved along, glancing into each of the cells to check that her magic still held. She couldn't risk their escape, not when she'd fought so hard for so many years to capture them.

Soon it would all be over.

She hobbled toward the end of the corridor where one final door remained, this one shut tight and held closed with not just one lock but six, each enchanted with her Bitter magic. A tiny, barred window granted the only hint of what lay behind the metal barricade.

Kierra heard the huffing breath from several feet away, smelled the sour, putrid stench before she reached the door.

She paused when she neared it, hearing something moving inside the cell.

Something terrifyingly large.

Her lips curled with delight.

"Hello, my darling," she said, dragging a caressing finger over the cold metal door.

She touched each lock to ensure the Bitter links still held firm.

A snort sounded from the other side. A gust of hot breath escaped the small window.

"There you are," Kierra said, raising up on tiptoes and talons to see inside.

Gigantic reptilian eyes blinked back at her, framed by scaled crocodilian skin. The ammit backed away, revealing huffing nostrils and a lion-shaped maw filled with glistening, yellow teeth. A mane of thick scaled spikes surrounded its horrid face. She couldn't even see the entirety of its hippopotamus-sized body through the tiny window.

"Are you hungry?" she cooed.

The ammit let out a low growl.

"There, there, no need to get testy. I've prepared a lovely meal for you, including a nice appetizer to hold you over. But you must be patient just a little while longer."

The ammit hissed.

Kierra inched back. This was the longest she'd ever kept it waiting for food. The ammit had surprising stamina and could go days without eating.

But it had been weeks since she last fed it.

Many weeks.

She could see the hunger in its eyes. Kierra took another step back, not liking the way the creature looked at her.

Like *she* would make a delicious meal.

"My crown?"

Kierra jumped and turned.

"Fia! What have I told you about sneaking up on me on those silent feet of yours? Announce yourself!"

"Yes, of course. Forgive me. It's just . . . I'm ready for you."

The queen straightened the skirts of her gown and receded down the hall, casting a final glance into the cells that held her prisoners. She passed the spiral staircase where she'd entered the lower level, then continued past it.

A low growl rumbled behind her. She turned before rounding a corner, smiling one more time in the direction of the most ferocious creature she'd ever made.

Kierra followed Fia through an arched doorway into a room that very few of her subjects knew existed. Admittedly, it felt a bit like a dungeon as well. Perhaps especially to the creatures she kept there.

Fia gestured, and Kierra crossed the stone floor toward a plush, blue velvet wingback chair in the center of the room and took her seat.

"I'll be right back," Fia said.

Kierra scanned the room while she waited.

A dozen cages lined the four stone walls, three on each side. But only two held anything: a large but sickly-looking stag in one, an ostrich in the other.

Fia returned a moment later, wheeling in a cart with a contraption on top made from glass beakers, funnels, tubes, and hollow copper wires. She unraveled one of the thin metal threads and stretched it toward Kierra, motioning for her to lift her sleeve.

Kierra obliged, nestling farther back into her seat.

Fia examined the queen's arm, then produced a small shaving razor from a pocket in her dress. She held it up, and Queen Kierra nodded.

Fia lowered the blade to Kierra's arm and shaved away a small patch of fur, then lifted the end of the thin metal tube where a copper needle glimmered in the torchlight.

She pricked Kierra's arm, then adjusted the needle until it remained in place.

"How is that, my crown?"

Kierra merely dipped her head in acknowledgment of the question.

Fia nodded, then strode across the room toward the stag. She opened the door to its cage, but the creature didn't move, head held low beneath the weight of its antlers.

"This will be the last treatment we can draw from the stag," Fia said.

Kierra scraped her gaze around the room. After tonight, only the ostrich would remain. "We can always find more," Kierra said.

Fia's voice quavered. "There aren't any more."

Kierra narrowed her cat eyes. "None?"

Fia shook her head. "Not a single creature left in the kingdom with the Eylan. Only the Reds and the other dogs you've recently captured from Yarou."

And the whole human and the Reds she travels with.

But Kierra didn't say it aloud.

Instead, surprise trickled through her veins as she considered Fia's words, the insight propelling her motives to expand her reign beyond this realm. But she merely said, "Then I've done my job well."

Still she wondered if it weren't possible they'd missed something: a rodent, a frog, a rabbit . . .

Kierra pondered what might happen once she could no longer derive her serums—or receive a direct infusion as she did now.

She would need the additional fuel to sustain her on her upcoming journey to Eblor. After seeing the toll her body had taken during her travels to Oorbara, she couldn't take any risks. She needed as much power as her body could hold at once.

Frustratingly, it wasn't much.

Which was why she'd created the serums and often kept creatures in captivity until she was ready for them.

More importantly, it was why she'd created the troves.

Two of which the girl had already compromised.

Kierra had felt the familiar surging drain on her power two nights ago and *knew*—knew it in her Bitter bones—that the trove in the Sea of Oorbara had been unleashed. The girl now traveled with a second eidolon. Which was why Kierra had altered her plans for the Reds and the other dogs she'd recently captured.

It was also why she'd sent a second drift of griffins back to Yarou along with a flight of saraphs to scorch the earth and ensure no other living creatures remained.

But they'd found nothing.

"The kingdom is secure at last," Fia said.

Kierra shifted in her seat, schooling her features into placidity so as not to allow her concerns to become visible on her face.

"Yes, secure at last," she said. "Which is why I need this infusion tonight. I leave in the morning to take the Reds somewhere far away, where they'll never again be a threat to us or this kingdom."

One side of Fia's mouth quirked up into a smile as she turned and unraveled another spool of the wire-thin copper tubing, a matching copper cuff on the end. She approached the stag, but it hardly gave her a second glance. She snapped the cuff around one of its legs, then took a seat on a small stool in the corner of the room.

Kierra's eyes traced the wires and coils, noting how the device stretched between them.

Connected them.

A thought occurred to her, something the griffin Thorne had said.

The girl—the whole human—was bonded to one of the Reds.

Kierra's mind whirled as she watched the first golden drop leech from the deer, pass through the copper tube, then drip into the first glass cylinder. Another drop quickly followed.

The device balanced the cylinder in a thin metal stand she'd designed to tip once the level had reached the top.

Kierra's eyes fixated on the liquid-light that dripped from the stag's veins. Her eyes flicked to the ostrich, who watched with a horrified expression, realizing it would be next.

The liquid passed the halfway point. The glass cylinder wobbled in the stand. The stag slumped against the wall.

Pain spread across Kierra's forehead, then a pounding, splitting ache.

She casually rested her head in her hand, not allowing Fia to see the look of excruciation on her face.

Or the fear.

Because though Kierra had very nearly rid the land of the Reds, a final threat remained.

A greater threat.

The girl.

And there was only one place left for her to go.

Which was why Kierra couldn't take any risks with the third trove.

Despite the securities she'd already put in place to hide and protect her greatest store of power, this time when the girl showed up, Kierra would be waiting.

She'd already discussed it with Makk, who helped her carefully devise a plan to take the Reds to the third trove and bind them there, leeching their power and fueling her third and final store.

Right before she killed the girl.

But as Kierra stared at the coils of copper and swirls of glass that connected her to the stag— *binding* her to it—she recalled what had happened in this room a few weeks ago with the White pup and adult Brown. Kierra smiled, considering a new twist to her plan.

She glanced up, seeing the glass fill to the brim. The weight of the liquid-light tipped the cylinder, dumping the contents into another glass container, this one with a funnel on the bottom. The first drop slipped through the small opening, then dripped into a coil of glass tubing she'd imbued with her Bitter magic to distill the animal's energy into her own. She watched as the first drop of black viscous Bitter dripped from the tip of the coil, then splattered into another glass cylinder. She shuddered at the thought of it hitting her veins.

In moments it would.

The Bitter liquid began to fill the second glass, drip by drip.

Several agonizingly slow minutes later, the liquid reached the tipping point. The cylinder wobbled in its stand, then tilted, dumping the contents into the final funnel that connected to the copper tube leading to Kierra's arm. A tingle of power washed over her as the serum seeped into her veins.

But this time, pain accompanied it. More than usual. She bit her lip, grimacing as she felt the newest nub of an antler break through the skin of her forehead. Hot liquid trickled down her face. She groaned, and Fia looked up. The human-hybrid rushed over, yanking a handkerchief from the pocket of her dress, and dabbed the queen's face. The same black Bitter—her blood—stained the cloth.

"Are you all right, my crown?"

Kierra drew in a sharp breath through her nostrils to steady her voice before saying, "I'll be fine. But please be sure to pack *all* of my belongings for my journey tomorrow." She gestured to the contraption of glass and copper coils. A scheming smile curled on her lips. "You never know when I might need it."

"Yes, my crown. I'll ensure it's packed, along with any serum we still have in reserve."

Kierra watched as the last trickles of golden power dripped into the device and cycled through to reach her veins.

The stag collapsed with a deafening thud. Its antlers clashed against the floor, and a final sigh escaped its lips.

The ostrich screeched.

Kierra stared at the dead deer as she pulled the needle from her arm, then tentatively reached up to touch the second antler on her forehead. The point was sharp, honed.

Just like her.

Just as she'd need to be to face the journey ahead and finally—fully—eliminate every single threat from her kingdom.

The story continues in

BOOK THREE

A TAIL OF MAGIC
AND LOVE

Get your copy at
hrhutzel.com

BEFORE YOU GO...

Thank you for reading Book Two in the Fable of Eylan series, *A Tail of Flame and Storm*!

As a thank you, I invite you to download a free digital album, featuring mesmerizing character art and magical scenes from the series.

Download it at
hrhutzel.com/lookbook

ENJOY THIS BOOK?

YOU CAN MAKE A BIG DIFFERENCE!

I am so grateful for my committed and loyal readers! Your reviews are some of the best thank-yous I can receive.

Reviews are the most powerful tool I have as an author when it comes to bringing my books to the attention of other readers.

If you enjoyed this book, I would be very grateful if you could spend just five minutes leaving a review (it can be as short as you like) on Amazon, Goodreads, or at my website hrhutzel.com/review-foe

JOIN MY READERS' CLUB TO CONNECT!

Get freebies, book updates, discounts, and more when you sign up. I'll meet you in your inbox!

Join at
hrhutzel.com/signup

ABOUT THE AUTHOR

After discovering the power of stories through her first bestselling novel, H. R. Hutzel has been on a journey to write inspirational stories that guide readers into the mystical realm within, where they can not only "lose themselves" between the pages but find themselves too.

Hutzel lives in Kentucky with her husband and beloved golden retrievers. She's an introvert by nature, an extrovert by necessity, and one of those delightful weirdos who's best understood by other weirdos—and dogs, of course! When she's not writing, you'll find her digging in the garden, walking with her pups, or hanging out in the hammock with a good book.

EMBRACING THE JOURNEY OF DOG OWNERSHIP

Throughout this book, we've celebrated the extraordinary love and bonds shared with our dogs. If you're inspired to welcome a dog into your life, it's a joyous decision that comes with a rewarding journey. Dogs bring unparalleled happiness and companionship, and they thrive with our attention and care.

As you consider becoming a dog owner, remember that adopting a dog is a lifelong partnership—one that requires a commitment to their happiness, health, and well-being. It's about being their forever home, offering consistent love, and embracing the responsibilities that come with nurturing their needs and ensuring their safety.

To support you in making an informed decision, I invite you to visit hrhutzel.com/dog-resources where I've compiled some of my favorite resources for dog-owners and those considering bringing a dog into their lives. These resources are designed to help ensure that you and your future furry friend create a joyful and nurturing lifelong bond.

Thank you for your thoughtful consideration and for spreading the magic of love, one wagging tail at a time!